The Wrong

CW00839601

This Armada book belongs to:

_____

_____

_____

The Chalet School series by Elinor M. Brent-Dyer

Above is a complete list of Chalet School titles though only those set in bold type are available in Armada paperbacks. Unfortunately we cannot keep all these titles in print simultaneously but an up-to-date stocklist can be sent on request.

Elinor M. Brent-Dyer

The Wrong
Chalet School

Armada

The Wrong Chalet School was first published in
the U.K. in 1952 by W. & R. Chambers Ltd, Edinburgh
This revised edition was first published in Armada in 1970 by
Fontana Paperbacks,
8 Grafton Street, London W1X 3LA

Armada is an imprint of
Fontana Paperbacks, part of
the Collins Publishing Group

This impression 1986

© Elinor M. Brent-Dyer 1925

Printed in Great Britain by
William Collins Sons & Co. Ltd, Glasgow

CHAPTER I

KATHARINE SETS OUT

KATHARINE stood on the platform at Paddington, looking round anxiously. It had been a most awful rush, but you expected that with Aunt Luce. She was a dear thing; but so vague!

When Mother had written to say that she wanted Katharine to go to a boarding-school now that she was fourteen, Aunt Luce had said, "Oh, of course! That school where her great friend used to be a mistress. Now where was it? The Chalet School! That was it! I'll write tomorrow."

Unfortunately, by the time tomorrow came, she had been seized with a fresh inspiration for a picture which drove everything else out of her head; and when, a week later, her niece asked casually what the school had said about having her, Aunt Luce had shrieked with horror. She had never thought of it again!

"How does one find out which school it is?" she had asked helplessly.

Eventually, she had written to an educational agency and discovered three Chalet Schools—one in Sussex; one on an island off the coast of South Wales; one at Tanswick in Pembrokeshire. To be on the safe side, all three were written to.

The Sussex one was only a preparatory, so of no use. Aunt Luce "swithered," to quote herself, between the other two, but fixed on one at last because she thought the uniform sounded good—brown and orange. The other one was brown and flame.

"And that," Aunt Luce said wisely, "may mean anything from crimson to lemon yellow. It's too vague."

No one seemed to know if Mrs Gordon's friend had taught at either and it was impossible to find out, for shortly after the letter had been sent off, word arrived that the big hospital in Central China where Dr and Mrs Gordon worked had been taken over by the Chinese Government and certain of the personnel had been arrested for "spying and subversive activities against the Government," among them, the Gordons. Since then nothing had been heard.

Aunt Luce, having written to make arrangements of a sort, had taken Katharine off to Brittany on a sketching tour, and it was not until her niece one day mentioned that term-time must be drawing near that Miss Gordon woke up to the fact that there was less than a week left before the girl had to be at Paddington to join the train for Tanswick.

The flurry that followed had been monumental. All Katharine's possessions and some of her aunt's had been tossed pell-mell into cases. They had headed for the nearest airport and, luckily, succeeded in booking the last two vacant seats on next day's plane for England. Since then they had sped from shop to shop, buying Katharine's outfit.

It is, perhaps, needless to say that the final letter from the Head of the school had been lost. All either Katharine or Miss Gordon could remember was that her name was Wilson.

Aunt Luce was quite unconcerned. She felt sure that between that and the uniform it would be quite easy to park Katharine with the right school. So far, however, they had not been successful.

"Aunt Luce, what shall we do?" Katharine suddenly asked desperately.

"Don't panic, child. It's quite simple. I'm certain we shall find the uniform easily. Brown and orange is very distinctive, you see. You'll join the girls and that will be that," Aunt Luce finished solemnly. Then she went off at a tangent. "I drew some money from the bank for you in case you should need more than your weekly pocket money. Here you are. I'm going back to Brittany to finish that big picture of Baie du Forêt. Then I may go south to the Pyrenees and Lourdes. Put it away and mind you remember what you've done with it!"

This from Aunt Luce, who was famed for never knowing where any of her possessions were at any given moment!

Katharine tucked away the little wad of notes and then looked round again. This time she was lucky. Standing in a little group at the nearer end of the platform were about a dozen schoolgirls wearing long brown coats and brown felt hats.

"Do you think those are them?" she asked Aunt Luce

eagerly. "They're the first *brown* uniforms we've seen here."

Miss Gordon gazed earnestly at them. "We might stroll along in that direction," she said. "Then we can see if they have any orange about them."

They strolled—and a swirling movement of one of the girls showed them such orange as was literally dazzling. Under the brown coat her tunic was bright reddish orange!

"*That's* not the school!" Aunt Luce said decidedly. 'It couldn't possibly be! I may have lost the letter and the prospectus, but I *know* the Head said *brown* tunics. This must be the flame-coloured school."

Katharine, who had been regarding the gaudy tunics with horror, fully agreed with this.

Once more they gazed round. Marching along the platform came a long string of girls, also in brown, and this time the coats gave glimpses of tunics to match.

"That's the one!" Aunt Luce proclaimed; and made a beeline for the tall young mistress in charge.

"This is the Chalet School, isn't it?" she demanded. "I've brought my niece Katharine Gordon who is joining you this term. Here she is!" pulling the suddenly shy Katharine forward.

The mistress gave Katharine a smiling glance before she looked quickly down the list she carried. "Mary Katharine Gordon. All correct!"

"I'm Katharine Mary," the owner of the name corrected her shyly.

"Someone at the office has slipped up, then. I have you down as Mary Katharine. Oh, well, I don't suppose it really matters. I'm Miss Burn, the Games mistress." She ticked the name on the list and turned to Miss Gordon. "That'll be all right, then. We're just going to take possession of our seats, so I expect you'd like to say good-bye." She called across to a tall, pretty girl who had been walking briskly along the train. "Found ours, Anthea?"

"Yes, Miss Burn. This carriage and about half the next."

"Good! Just begin seeing the girls in, will you?"

Anthea promptly swung open a door, and the rest, at a nod from Miss Burn, marched smartly across the platform and began taking their places in an orderly way that impressed Miss Gordon deeply and was in direct contrast to the other brown group, where the girls were pushing in with squeals and scrambling.

Miss Burn turned to the Gordon pair again. "I must just see to the Juniors, Miss Gordon. I'll do that while you and Katharine are saying good-bye and then come back for her. Thank you so much for bringing her on time."

She hurried after the girls, and Katharine suddenly realising that Aunt Luce's departure meant that she was going to be very much on her own in England for the next two or three months, turned to that lady with rather a stricken expression.

"Well, Katt, this'll be good-bye until July, anyhow," Aunt Luce said briskly. "I'll be at the Soleil d'Or for the next week or two; but I ought to have finished my picture by then, so I'll push on. I don't know what address to give you, I'm sure. I rather think of going to Lourdes and then crossing into Spain. I'd like to see Andorra. Anyway, I'll write. If you really need me at any time, I suppose the bank would send a letter on."

"O.K. But don't worry about me. I can stand on my own feet," Katharine said cheerfully.

Aunt Luce nodded. Suddenly she lowered her voice, and the blue Gordon eyes which Katharine, too, had inherited, were very blue. "Katt, don't worry if you don't hear from China just yet. It'll take time to get news through."

"I'm not *going* to worry," Katharine said firmly. "Daddy's always said it's a mug's game and doesn't help anyone. He told me that if I came to a sticky patch to talk to God about it and He'd always help, if only I'd faith and patience to wait. I've done the talking so now I'm going to wait."

"Well, that's all, I think," Miss Gordon said vaguely. "Oh, here's that mistress coming back. I like her face—it would make an interesting study, even though she is so pretty according to ordinary standards. There's something more to her than curly hair and really quite beautiful grey eyes. Well, good-bye, Katt. Don't forget; you can always get at me through the bank."

She gave her niece a quick peck and slipped away, largely because she felt on the verge of tears. The girl's unquestioning faith made her realise what sorrow might lie before them in the near future.

"Why—has your aunt gone?" Miss Burn asked in surprise when Katharine went up to her alone.

"Yes! she's flying back to Brittany on the next plane," Katharine explained. "She only came over to see me off."

8

She was too accustomed to Aunt Luce's erratic behaviour to think anything about it. Miss Burn accepted the explanation and took the new girl to a compartment where half a dozen girls of the same age were busily settling themselves.

"Now then, you folk," she said. "Aren't you settled *yet*? Hilary Wilson, this is Katharine Gordon. Look after her, please."

She gave them a smiling nod, pushed Katharine gently into the compartment and left them.

Hilary, a leggy fourteen-year-old, whose round pink-and-white face wore a perpetually cheeky look owing, as its owner used to say aggrievedly, to a pert nose; which meant that she could never get away with *anything*, bestowed a welcoming grin on the newcomer.

"Come on and squeeze in," she invited. "Shove up, Meg. You needn't take up two-thirds of the seat, even if you are as big again as most of us!"

"That's a libel," complained Meg, a plump young person of the same age. "Can you squash in here, Katharine? O.K. then. Heave your case up on the rack and squat."

"Isn't it rather huge for an overnight case?" asked a fair-haired damsel, coming to help with it.

"Well, it is; but you see we were in Brittany and Aunt Luce forgot all about school till the end of last week, so we had a frantic rush round and quite a lot got left out of my trunk, so she said I must just have a larger case and bring it with me," Katharine explained as they rammed the case home.

"Brittany?" Meg exclaimed. "Oh, you lucky object! What a smashing holiday;"

"Aunt Luce went to sketch—she's an artist," Katharine replied, feeling that she was doing rather a lot of explaining.

"Oh, I see." Meg subsided and turned to make a remark to her neighbour while Hilary, as the eldest of them, having seen that they were more or less settled at last, dropped into her own corner.

The girls were friendly enough, but naturally they had plenty of common interests to discuss and Katharine sat quietly, taking it all in and saying nothing.

Presently the fair girl, who was addressed as "Hilda" by the rest, observed, "I wonder if we'll have a regatta this term like last year?"

"Oh, I hope so! Remember the tub race?"

All collapsed into wild giggles at this reminder which came from Meg.

"*And* Mary-Lou winning from Clem Barrass?" Hilary supplemented. She turned to Katharine. "Do you row—or swim?" she asked.

Katharine laughed. "I've been told I could swim almost as soon as I could walk. We lived in Samoa then, and all the children are in and out of the water all day long. I can row a little, too."

"Did you learn that in Samoa as well?" someone else asked.

"No; we left there when I was six. Daddy got an appointment to the hospital in Singapore and Mother brought me home so I could go to an English school. I've lived with Aunt Luce since then—more or less, that is."

"What *do* you mean?" Hilda asked curiously.

"Well, Granny was alive at first and Aunt Luce wasn't always at home. But Gran died two years ago."

"I say," Hilary interrupted, "you *don't* mean that your Aunt Luce is the Lucia Gordon who had a one-man show last summer? Not really? Dad took Mummy and me to see them. I thought them smashing!"

Katharine flushed. "They say she's not bad," she said, trying to keep the pride out of her voice.

Someone else had been thinking. A pretty, dark girl, younger than the rest, whose father worked in the Admiralty, had been remembering various remarks she had overheard from the elders. "Is your father Dr John Gordon, then?" she asked gently.

Katharine nodded.

Elinor Pennell gave her a fleeting glance. "Have you—I don't want to poke and pry—but—is there any news yet?"

"Not so far." Katharine gave her a straight look. "How d'you know?"

"I've heard my people talking. Father's in the Admiralty. I say," Elinor interrupted herself as she glanced at her watch, "it's twelve now. What about eats?"

The attention was promptly turned from Katharine.

"Good idea!" Hilda approved the suggestion. "What've you got, everyone? Mother splashed and gave me tongue sandwiches."

Cases were hastily hauled down and opened, and packets of sandwiches, cakes, biscuits, tarts and sweets were produced with a variety of drinks from milk to ginger beer. Only Katharine had nothing, Aunt Luce having imagined that the girls would go to the restaurant-car for lunch.

"Don't bother," Hilda said cheerfully, seeing her hot cheeks as she produced the big packet of chocolate which was all she had. "The rest of us have heaps more than we can possibly manage and we always pool and share. Have one of these."

Katharine felt shy about it at first, but the rest pressed sandwiches and other food on her with such goodwill that by the time they were ready to share her chocolate she had forgotten her discomfort. When they finally tumbled out of the train at Cardiff she was beginning to feel that her school would be a success.

"There's that queer school!" Hilary remarked as they formed into lines. "Oh, I say!" as one of the girls turned and the flaming orange of her tunic showed under her coat. "Just look at *that*! What ghastly sights they must look without their coats!"

"Cheerful on a rainy day," Elinor Pennell suggested.

"What school is it?" Katharine asked interestedly as they marched over to join the lines.

"Believe it or not, it's *another* Chalet School," Hilda said with a giggle. "They used to be quite ordinary; but last year they had a new Head and she has the maddest ideas. She believes in you learning *what* you like and *when* you like. It *sounds* very nice, but I think it must be an awfully untidy way of doing things. I'd a lot rather do as we do and have time-tables."

"Buck up, there!" Hilary said. "Miss Burn is waving wildly at us—we're the last. Come on!"

They fled along the platform. Old pupils of the school knew that Hilary Burn was charming at most times; but get into her bad books and, as Meg Whyte said rather ruefully, you knew *all* about it!

The train for Swansea was in and they had to hurry, so that in the excitement, Katharine forgot all about the other Chalet School. She thoroughly enjoyed the journey, for the set she was with were very jolly girls and quite ready to be friendly.

At Swansea they left the train and crowded into motor-coaches and were driven to Carnbach, where ferries were waiting to take them across the Sound to St Briavel's, the

11

island on which the Chalet School was situated at present. It was a lovely evening and Katharine snuffed the fresh sea air delightedly. She felt thankful that Aunt Luce had pitched on *this* Chalet School and not the other. Like Meg, she felt that it would be much easier to work to time-table and not be left to your own devices.

"I'm going to enjoy this," she thought, as she paired off with Hilary for the walk from the ferry-landing to school.

CHAPTER II

"WHERE IS YOUR TRUNK?"

HILARY explained that they were allowed to talk quietly on the way to school.

"It wouldn't do if we all yelled at the tops of our voices," she said. "The inhabitants are used to us after a year, but there are visitors too. Anyhow, with all our crowd, it would be an *awful* din. It's wizard living on an island, you know."

"Not always," put in the girl behind her. "It can be a frantic bore if we want to go to the mainland and the ferries aren't running because of fog or wind or something."

"That doesn't often happen," Hilary said airily.

"Remember when Mrs Maynard was teaching the term before last and couldn't come for days because of that awful gale?"

"And then she did come and *stayed* for days," Hilary capped this. "It cuts both ways. Don't be such a grouch, Jennifer! Anyway, *that* won't matter this term," she added with a gusty sigh. "She won't be here at all!"

"Won't be here? Why on earth not?" Jennifer demanded.

"Don't you know? She's gone to Canada to join Lady Russell and taken all the kids with her. We shan't see her for ages—probably not until next term."

"How utterly petrifying!"

"Who is Mrs Maynard?" Katharine asked curiously, since the news seemed to have rendered Jennifer dumb.

Hilary gave her a sideways look. "She's Lady Russell's sister," she said.

"Who is Lady Russell?" Katharine felt bewildered.

Hilary explained. "The school belongs to Lady Russell and when she began it—in Tirol, that was—she was its Head. Then she married Dr Jem—he hadn't got his title then—and her partner Mlle Lepartre was Head. *She* got ill, so Miss Annersley, who was Senior Mistress, took over; and later Miss Wilson, who was the next Senior Mistress, came along, so we have two Heads."

This relieved Katharine, who had been beginning to feel that there must be some mistake somewhere, since she knew that the Head who had written to Aunt Luce was Miss Wilson.

"What about Mrs Maynard, though?" she asked.

"Oh, she was a kid at school—younger than us, I believe. She was Joey Bettany then. When she grew up she married Dr Maynard, who was one of the doctors at the San Dr Jem was running at the Sonnalpe. She has squads of kids, but even that doesn't make any difference, somehow. She says she still belongs to the school and always will."

Katharine had caught a name which was familiar. "Joey Bettany did you say? You surely don't mean—oh, but that would be a most fearful coincidence!"

"If what you're getting at is, is she Josephine M. Bettany the authoress," said Elinor Pennell who was in front, "you've got it in one. She is!"

"Oh, *no*! How—utterly—*spiffing*!" In her excitement Katharine had to fall back on the slang of her father's schooldays.

It was quite well received by those who heard her and to whom it was new. They adopted it forthwith, having been severely lectured for their too frequent use of current slang the term before, and until the prefects put their collective feet down, it was used almost monotonously by Upper Fourth when they wanted to use a superlative.

At the moment, they concentrated on their beloved Jo Bettany.

"She's one of my favourite writers," Katharine declared. "How simply marvellous to come to *her* school! But—did you say she won't be here all this term?"

"Well, she doesn't actually *live* at the school," Hilary explained. "They have Plas Gwyn outside of Howells village which is where we really ought to be. The drains at Plas Howell, which is the school, went bad on us a year ago last term, so they took them up and then found they were a lot more wrong than anyone had ever thought. I believe the place isn't right yet."

"So then, Meg, who was walking with Elinor, chimed in, "they had to find somewhere for us in the meantime and they found the Big House here. We'll go back to Plas Howell, of course, when it's all right again. Meanwhile, we haven't any objection to living on an island for a change."

"Well," Hilary took up the tale, "shortly after that—well, not quite shortly. It didn't happen till the Christmas term, actually—they found that something was awfully wrong with the foundations of Plas Gwyn—that's their house. So Dr Maynard took a house at Carnbach that belongs to Dickie Christy's father—Who's Dickie?" at Katharine's startled look. "She's one of the prefects. Real name's Delicia, but *can* you imagine anyone using a thing like that for everyday?"

"I can *not*!" Katharine spoke with emphasis.

"Nor me! Everyone calls her Dickie—even the Staff. Where was I? Oh—well, the Maynards moved to Carnbach and there they must stay until Plas Gwyn is safe again. We were awfully glad, for we missed her horribly that first term. Somehow, Joey seems to be a kind of foundation stone in the school! That's why it is so sick-making that we shan't have her at all the whole of this term."

"But *why* has she gone to Canada?" Jennifer demanded.

"I don't know. Because she wanted to, I suppose. She's taken the whole family with her, including Len and Con.

"But how do *you* know all this?" Meg asked.

"Because we met the whole crowd when we were in Southampton one day last week. They were sailing the next day and we went to see them off. Dr Jack had gone on—he was flying. Jo said she didn't fancy flying with a whole mob of kids—she's taken Sybil Russell as well—so they were going by boat."

"Sybil gone as well? Then who on earth's going to be form prefect this term?" Meg demanded in consternation.

"Not an earthly! I suppose we'll hear tomorrow. Sybs was dancing with excitement. She'll see those new twins of theirs at last."

"So she will. She's being dying for that ever since they arrived. Hello! Here we are," Meg said, as the long lines swung in at a wide-open gate and marched smartly up a paved path between high hedges of closely-cut holly.

"You'll see the house in a minute, Katharine. We're nearly at the end of this."

A minute later the path and the hedges ended in a gate of ornamental ironwork, and Katharine saw great lawns spreading out on either hand, with beds and borders filled with spring flowers and, straight ahead, a big old house dating back to the early eighteenth century. The wide door was in the middle, with rows of windows on either hand, and more rows above. The house had been newly white-washed, and already a climbing rose was flinging a veil of young green across the walls, springing right up to the slated roof, which was steeply pitched with serried rows of dormer windows.

The ground-floor windows varied in style, some of them being quaint old bow windows, while others, cut later, were french windows, opening on to the lawn. Two rows running above were sash windows flung wide now so that the sweet salt air could sweep through the dormitories.

So much Katharine saw. Then two people appeared in the wide doorway and the girls sped up the drive to meet them.

The taller of the ladies held out her hands to fend off the rush and the girls were quiet at once. Evidently discipline was good though there was no sense of repression.

"Well, girls," said the other briskly. "Welcome back! Had good holidays?"

There was only one answer to this and it was given with enthusiasm, followed by a request to know if the Heads had also enjoyed themselves. They were told that though short, the holiday had been excellent. Then they were called to order and sent to stand in their various forms on the lawns. Katharine found herself alone on the drive and both felt and looked self-conscious.

The tall mistress nodded to her pleasantly. "Mary Katharine Gordon, I know. Who is looking after you?"

"I am, Miss Wilson," Hilary spoke up quickly, beckoning to the new girl to join their line.

"Good! Go with Hilary now, and tomorrow we'll find out just which form is likely to be yours. Look after her, Hilary."

"Yes, Miss Wilson," Hilary said demurely. "Come and stand by me, Katharine."

Katharine went, wondering if she ought to explain at

once the mistake that had been made in her name. Further, she was rather startled that Miss Wilson seemed to know who she was. However, that was explained next moment by the other mistress whom the girls had addressed as "Miss Annersley."

"You are the last of our new girls for this term, Katharine. The other three came by the earlier ferry."

"Now, girls," Miss Wilson said, "supper will be ready in about twenty minutes. Go to the splasheries and change your shoes before you take your cases upstairs and tidy. *Some* of you seem to stand in much need of a wash," she added with a clear laugh. "Off you go! We'll meet again at Abendessen."

Wondering what on earth this meant, Katharine meekly went with Hilary when they marched off round the house to a side-door where they separated, the Juniors going in one direction, the Seniors vanishing through a baize-covered door, while Hilary and her crowd led the way into a small, rather dark room with pegs round three of the walls and lockers beneath them. Stands ran down the centre of the room with more pegs and lockers, and at the remaining side were five toilet basins.

Some of the pegs were already occupied and Katharine was startled to notice that these had a small hook beneath the coat peg on which hung a towel.

"This is our form's splashery," Hilary explained. "Yes; I thought so. Here's your name next to mine—at least, I suppose 'M. K. Gordon's' your name?" she added doubtfully.

"Yes—but they've got it the wrong way round," Katharine said. "I'm Katharine Mary; not Mary Katharine."

"Oh, well, it doesn't really matter, does it? Hang up your hat and coat and change—oh, but I suppose your slippers are at the bottom of your case, so you can't. Well, hang on a sec while *I* change, anyhow."

Hilary pulled a pair of slippers out of her locker and changed from her stout walking shoes rapidly. Then she stood up. "Ready! Come on; we've got to go and find Matey and see which is your dormy. This way!"

She led Katharine up uncarpeted stairs at the back of the house and there, standing at the head, was a small, wiry-looking woman whose nurse's uniform was immacu-

16

late and who, as Katharine later wrote to Aunt Luce, simply crackled with starch.

"Good evening, Matron," Hilary said very properly. "This is Katharine Gordon. Which dormitory is she in, please?"

Matron glanced down the sheaf of typed lists she held and found the name at once. "Yours, Hilary. I suppose you know that Sybil Russell has gone to Canada to join her mother and won't be here this term. I've put— Katharine, is it?—in her cubicle for the time being. Take her along and hurry up, both of you."

Hilary stood not on the order of her going. Towing Katharine along, she sped down the corridor to a staircase at the other end, up that and into another wide corridor, down which she went till they came to an open door half-way along. She led her charge into a big, airy room, looking over an orchard which was a sea of rosy apple blossom beyond which a glimpse of the darkening sea could be obtained. Three wide windows lit it along one side and it was criss-crossed by iron rods on six-foot standards, from which hung pretty curtains patterned with twists and trails of green leaves on a cream ground.

"This is 'Leafy'," Hilary explained as she drew Katharine towards a cubicle at the far end. "You're lucky to have Sybil's cubey. It shares my window, you see." She nodded towards the next-door one and Katharine's face lit up as she realised that the dividing rod gave them each half a window.

"How awfully jolly," she said. "Lattice windows, too."

Hilary nodded. "I like them better than the sash ones. Anyhow, it's only the Juniors that have those. All these side dormies and the back ones, too, have lattices. Now, Katharine, there's precious little time. Dump your case and get your brush and comb out and tidy your hair. If you *can* fish for your slippers, it might be a good move. Bag your towel when you're ready and we'll go down to the Splash and wash. We are supposed to use the bathrooms during the day. Drop your curtains, by the way."

She vanished into the next-door cubicle, pulling down the dividing curtain after her, and Katharine made haste to draw the other two.

There was little time to take note of her surroundings. She rummaged in her bag for her keys, opened her case, and after some fishing found her slippers, a face-towel

17

and soap, brush and comb and her hand-mirror. Three minutes were spent on the long hair she wore plaited half-way down in two pigtails which dangled on either side of her face. Then she changed her shoes, setting them neatly under her bed, and went to open the dividing curtain and summon Hilary.

That young woman was just ready. She came through and glanced round the cubicle.

"Where's your shoes?" she demanded.

"Under my bed. I wondered if I ought to leave them there."

Hilary dived under the pretty counterpane that matched the curtains and picked them up. "I'll say not! I should have told you, though. Come on!"

"'I feel like 'Alice' and 'The Red Queen'," Katharine thought with some humour as she followed Hilary from the room. "I'm being told 'Come on!' so much."

They went back to the splashery where, by dint of elbowing and shoving, Hilary made room for them both at one of the basins and they washed. She showed the new girl the tiny hook beneath her coat-peg to hang up her towel. Then she marched her off just as a booming sound brought girls from every hole and corner as it seemed to Katharine, to join a long line which was proceeding in orderly fashion along the corridor.

The line wound into the big school dining-room where Hilary seated her charge next herself and saw to her wants, keeping up a series of conversations with about half a dozen other people at the same time.

She managed to say hurriedly to the new girl, "First night, no rules. *And* talk in any language you like."

Katharine gasped at the last remark. Whatever language did they expect her to use? However, Hilary was describing her meeting with the Maynards to several interested people, so she said nothing but went on with her supper.

No mistresses were present, but a certain amount of order was kept by the big girls, one of whom, a very fair, very pretty person, tapped a bell when the room grew too noisy.

"That's Peggy Bettany, the Head Girl," Hilary explained, when her tale was ended and the rest were discussing something else for the moment. "Sybil Russell told me this was to be her last term here. Next term, they're

18

opening some kind of annexe in Switzerland where prefects and sixth-formers who want to can go for their last year. Peggy's going, lucky wretch! So's Mollie Carewe and Barbara Henschell and Joan Sandys—oh, and quite half of that crowd, I expect. Mother says if I work hard enough to make it worth while, she and Daddy would think of it for me when *I'm* seventeen."

At this point, Peggy banged firmly on her bell for silence and when she got it, the girls rose for Grace, after which the Head Girl told all present to go to their common-rooms and wait until they were called for unpacking.

"Prayers will be at half-past seven tonight," she said in the clear, silvery voice that, to Katharine's thinking, just matched her appearance. "After Prayers, everyone under thirteen will go to bed. Under-sixteens go at half-past eight and the rest at half-past nine. Clear, please!"

On the word, every girl seized her plate, spoon and fork, napkin and glass and then they marched, table after table, to the hatch where they deposited everything to be collected by the pleasant-looking maids waiting there, except for the napkins, which were put into deep, narrow baskets standing on the sideboard at the side of the hatch.

That done, the girls left the room and streamed off to the common-rooms where, as was explained to the new girls, their free time was passed in bad weather.

"Not that we shall see much of them this term," a puckish-looking girl of fifteen remarked. "At least, we hope not. We shall be out of doors most of the time, thank goodness!"

"Rowing, this term!" added someone else.

"*And* swimming!" Hilary chimed in.

What else might have been said Katharine never knew, for at that moment the door opened and one of the prefects came in, called for silence and, when she had got it, said, "The following are to go to Matron now—Hilary Wilson—Hilda Jukes—Jean Ackroyd—Carola Johnston —Freda Lund—Vanna Ozanne—and the new girl, Katharine Gordon. Hurry up; and please go quietly."

"Unpacking!" Hilary exclaimed. "Come along, Katharine!"

They hurried upstairs to where Matron was waiting in what was known as "the trunk-room," together with some of the Senior girls. She quickly assigned each of the others to a Senior and then turned to Katharine.

"Come outside a moment, please, Katharine. Dicky, keep order while I'm gone."

"Yes, Matron," Dicky said as she turned to pick up Hilary's inventory from the tray of the trunk.

Matron led the way, shut the door behind her and Katharine, who was wondering what *could* be wrong, and then demanded crisply: "And now, I want to know where is your trunk?"

CHAPTER III

FIRST NIGHT

KATHARINE gaped at Matron on hearing this question.

"Well?" that lady said impatiently. "What has happened to your trunk? I suppose it was sent off a week ago like all the rest?"

The new girl pulled herself together. "N-not exactly," she stammered. "I—I mean it was only sent off two days ago."

Matron said nothing—and said it eloquently. Katharine had already been told that she could make you shake in your shoes with a mere look when she liked. Now she was looking, and the new girl didn't like it.

"You'd best come to my room and we'll get to the bottom of all this," the little lady said finally. She opened the door of the trunk-room. "Dickie, I have to deal with something at once. Here is my list. Finish this set and then send for the next lot if I haven't returned by then."

"Yes, Matron," the big, pleasant-faced seventeen-year-old girl replied promptly.

"Thank you. This way, Katharine."

She led the way downstairs to the next corridor where she took Katharine to a charming bed-sitting-room. She plumped down at the desk set near the window and waved her new subject to the window seat. Katharine sat down and waited.

"Now then! Why was your trunk not sent off last

week? It is stated quite plainly in the prospectus that all trunks should be sent a week in advance."

"We were in Brittany and Aunt Luce forgot about school until the end of the week," Katharine explained.

"Good Heavens!" Matron was silent for a moment. Then she demanded, "Well, do you know if it was sent by rail or road?"

"By rail—luggage in advance."

"And that was the day before yesterday? H'm! Well, it *might* be here by the end of the week, I suppose. Meantime, we must see what you're lacking. Sheets and pillow-cases, of course. I'd best give you some from Emergency and you can make your bed up now as you can't unpack."

"Yes, Matron," Katharine responded meekly.

"Wait here a moment."

Matron rose and left the room to return a few minutes later with sheets and pillow-cases which she laid down.

"How did you manage to wash before tea?" she inquired.

"Aunt Luce had forgotten to buy the face-towels until after the trunk had gone so I had to bring them with me," Katharine explained, wishing, not for the first time, that Aunt Luce were a little more like other folk. "There were some other things, too. That's why I had to bring such a huge case."

"I'd best come and see what you *have* brought," Matron decided, bundling sheets and pillow-cases into Katharine's arms before she turned to the desk to pick up a tablet and a fountain pen. "Come along to your dormitory."

Katharine followed her to the dormitory, where four girls were busy putting away their belongings. There was a good deal of noise going on, but Matron only laughed as she led the way and remarked, 'It's well for you people that this is first night! Hurry up and finish!'"

In the pretty cubicle, Katharine had first to make her bed, with Matron giving her a hand and showing her the one way she approved for bed-making. Then she had to pull her suitcase from under the bed and unpack it.

Blouses, beret, Sunday coat and skirt, pyjamas, bedroom slippers and dressing-gown as well as the more usual things came out of it. There were two more face-towels, handkerchiefs and a pair of stockings. Finally, under the extra underthings Aunt Luce had suddenly added the day before, an enormous box of chocolates emerged.

21

These Matron confiscated with the remark, "These must go to the sweet cupboard and you may have two or three every day. Hang that coat and skirt up in the cupboard—you'll find the pegs marked with your name. Dressing-gown and bedroom slippers *here*; handkerchiefs and other oddments in *this* drawer and the blouses in the one below. Underclothes in the next and your pyjamas on the bed. I'll take the towels to the linen-room. The beret goes to your splashery. Lay those photos on the shelf behind your bed and you can arrange them later. That all? Then give me the towels and bring the case along. Are these all marked, by the way?"

Katharine, who had sat for ages marking her possessions neatly with marking-ink, replied that they were, and showed them. That, however, was not at all the right thing, she found. They should have had name-tapes.

"Are *all* your belongings marked in ink?" Matron demanded.

Katharine went red. "There wasn't time to order name-tapes," she said.

Matron looked at her. "What *was* your aunt thinking about to leave things so late?" she demanded accusingly.

"She's an artist, you see," the new girl explained rather helplessly.

Matron groaned. "Oh, one of *that* kind! Very well; it isn't your fault. I'll order the name-tapes and you can sew them on during your first two or three needlework lessons. I'll speak to Mlle Berné or whoever takes you. Bring that case along and then you had best go back to the common-room. Can you find it, do you think? Someone will show you if you aren't sure."

"I can find it, thank you."

"Very well. By the way, who's in charge of you?"

Katharine gaped at her. Then she suddenly realised what was meant and replied, "Hilary Wilson."

Matron drew her mouth down in a comical grimace. "Who was responsible for that, I'd like to know? Well, she's a nice child, but don't let her drag you into her monkey tricks. Set that case down in the corner and go and find the common-room."

While she had been talking, Matron had bustled Katharine upstairs again. Now she vanished into the trunk-room and there was nothing for the new girl to do but put her case down and then go down to the common-

22

room where she found Hilary and Co. sitting, talking hard, having already finished unpacking.

"Hello!" Hilary said, as the new girl came rather shyly into the room. "Finished? You've been jolly quick, haven't you? Why did Matey want you?"

"To see what I had in my case and to ask why my trunk hadn't come yet," Katharine explained in subdued tones.

Hilary glanced at her quickly. It was early days for a girl of fourteen to begin being homesick. Katharine caught her look and guessed what she was thinking.

"I'm rather bothered about my trunk," she explained.

By this time, the information had seeped through to the others and they all stared at her in amazement.

"You mean to say your trunk hasn't come?" Hilda Jukes exclaimed. "Why, when was it sent off?"

"The day before yesterday. You see, Aunt Luce had forgotten all about term beginning——"

"*What?*" It came as a chorus.

"She's like that. It's being an artist, I expect," the lady's niece said defensively.

A girl a little older than herself, who had been standing at the back of the crowd, nodded. "*Don't I* know it!"

Hilary began to laugh. "If anyone does, you certainly ought to, Clem. Katharine, this is Clem Barrass, and *both* her parents are artists!"

Katharine looked at the charming, irregular face with its red-brown eyes just matching the colour of the plaits dangling down her back, and the white even teeth she showed when she smiled, and liked her on sight.

Clem nodded to her in a friendly way. "It's exactly the sort of thing Mum does. I've always had to look after the family or we should have been well in the soup more than once, I promise you. Don't worry, Katharine. The trunk'll turn up and we'll all rally round if you need anything until it does." She broke off to address a blue-eyed Junior who had strolled into the room just then. "Well, Mary-Lou? What do *you* want?"

"I can't find my white socks," Mary-Lou explained. "Are they with your things, Clem?"

"Certainly *not*! Auntie Doris gave them to you to put in just before your trunk was locked. What did you do with them?" Clem demanded.

Mary-Lou thought, nibbling at the end of one of the

fair pigtails she sported. "I don't know. Yes, though; I do! Don't you remember? Auntie Jo rang up to say goodbye and I dropped them down somewhere and ran. I never thought of them again till I couldn't find them just now and Peggy Bettany sent me to ask if they'd been put into your trunk. She's been unpacking me."

"Where were you when the 'phone went?" Clem asked sternly.

"In the spare room. I'd gone to fetch my hanks as well." Mary-Lou began to giggle. "I s'pôse they'e all there somewhere. I'm not sure, but I rather think I chucked them into an open drawer."

"Mary-Lou! You really *are*!" Clem spoke more in sorrow than in anger. "Bill told me I could go and ring Auntie Doris at seven and let her know we'd arrived safely, so I'll tell her and ask her to look for them and post them on. All right, you can trot off now and tell Peggy that I'm seeing to it."

"Mind you give Mother my love," Mary-Lou responded cheerfully before she skipped off again.

The elder girls looked at each other and laughed.

"Isn't that Mary-Lou all over?" Elinor Pennell said.

" 'Casual' doesn't begin to describe her," Clem agreed.

"What is her real name?" Katharine asked curiously.

"Mary Louise, but no one ever calls her anything but Mary-Lou," Clem replied. "My kid brother and I live with the Trelawneys in holiday times because Mother and Dad have gone off abroad on a sketching tour. I keep an eye on Mary-Lou in term-time and it's a hard life, I can tell you!"

Another bunch of girls came in just then so the matter dropped. All the same, Katharine felt attracted to both Clem and Mary-Lou.

Being a new girl, she kept herself modestly in the background and began to form opinions about her new comrades. She liked Hilary who had befriended her, and her fat chum, Meg Whyte. She liked slim, dark Elinor Pennell and, in a lesser degree, Hilda Jukes, who seemed to be on the gigglesome side. She thought Jennifer Penrose was something of a whiner and there were one or two girls who held no attraction for her. On the whole, however, she felt that she could be happy here.

Her thoughts were interrupted by the bell ringing for Prayers, by which time, most people were unpacked. The

24

noise and chatter which had been growing steadily ceased magically; the girls formed into two lines and, when a second bell rang, marched off smartly.

Katharine had not been overlooked. After the first bell Hilary had come to her and asked quietly, "Are you Protestant or R.C.?"

"Church of England, I suppose," Katharine told her, staring. "Why?"

"Because we divide for Prayers. I'm C. of E. myself, so you'd better keep with me. Miss Annersley takes our Prayers and Bill—I mean," in some confusion, "Miss Wilson—has the Catholics because she is one. There's the silence bell. Stand with me."

They went to Big Hall, a great room that had once been the double drawing-room at the Big House. Here they took their places, Kindergarten and Juniors in front, Sixth Form at the back, the rest standing between them in order of form. At one side of the dais at the head of the room sat the prefects, a most select body, with the choir facing them, as Hilary explained, once they were in their places, waiting for the Staff.

Katharine looked eagerly at the top door when the final bell sounded. She was very curious to see the mistresses. They streamed in, looking very fresh and attractive in their pretty dresses. Many of them were much younger than she had expected, though three or four were clearly contemporaries of the mistresses at her last school. Miss Burn was there, coming in with a small fair young woman, who was characterised by a very firm mouth.

Hilary murmured softly, "Miss Edwardes with Burnie. Miss Alton at the piano—she takes the Kinders——" She stopped short, for Miss Annersley had swept in and one of Lower Fifth B., standing immediately behind them, had given her a poke.

When the Head was standing at the lectern, pretty Peggy Bettany rose in her seat at the head of the prefects and announced the hymn. Katharine noticed that her silvery voice reached to the farthest corner of the great room, though she seemed to make no attempt to raise it. Miss Alton at the piano struck a chord and the beginning-of-term hymn swelled out, sung by well over a hundred young voices with excellent support from the Staff. The parable of the Talents followed and then they knelt for Prayers.

When they sat down again after the Blessing, a door at the back of the room opened and the rest of the girls marched in and took their places with their various forms, the Catholic mistresses joining their peers on the dais.

Katharine watched the long lines filling up and felt puzzled. She had had an idea that her new school was not much larger than her prep. She had no means of counting, but it struck her that there must be at least two hundred girls here, and probably more.

"Aunt Luce again!" she thought resignedly.

"Sit down, girls," Miss Annersley said quietly to a group of Middles who seemed to be scrimmaging for places.

They took their seats in rather more orderly fashion then, and Katharine saw that Mary-Lou Trelawney was among them and that she took her seat with a decided fling of the fair plaits that came midway to her waist. A little girl of the same age followed her into the row and sat down with a flounce that spoke volumes to the onlooker.

"Phil Craven—a pest of a kid!" Meg Whyte on Katharine's other side murmured, indicating the last-mentioned young person with a wag of her head. Then she stopped, for one of the mistresses was glaring at her meaningly.

The Staff sat down and Miss Annersley leant on the reading-desk and surveyed the girls with smiling eyes.

"Welcome back, everyone," she said. "We hope this will be a very happy term for everyone—including the exam. people."

She paused as the girls broke into laughter at this, and sundry people among the Seniors pulled long faces. Then she held up her hand and they were silent again.

"We won't talk about exams. just now," she went on. "Instead, I want to remind you all that this is the summer term, so we shall have tennis and cricket as usual. Miss Burn tells me that the tennis courts are ready and so is the cricket ground. The boats are all in trim and you will have your boating and swimming lessons as soon as possible. I must remind you all that no one may go boating who is unable to swim at least a hundred yards. So if any Middles or Seniors want to learn to row and are not up to that standard, I advise them to work hard at their swimming."

She turned with a smile to Miss Burn, who rose to the

26

occasion at once with "We're hoping to be able to manage three swimming periods a week for everyone this term, Miss Annersley."

There was clapping at this which subsided as the Head continued: "This is the term we have our special expedition in honour of Madame's birthday. I'm afraid we can't hope to have her with us—nor Mrs Maynard—'Joey' still to so many of you!—since she has sailed for Canada and we are not very likely to see her again before next term."

A groan went round the room at this. Katharine gathered that what Hilary and the rest had told her was true, that Mrs Maynard was regarded as a vital part of the school, married though she might be.

Miss Annersley smiled sympathetically. "Yes, girls; I know it's very trying. All the same, I think it's just as well for us to lose our blessings for a while sometimes, just to teach us to value them more highly. Besides, Joey told me when she came to say good-bye that she fully expected to get at least *three* books out of this trip, so we must all look forward to that."

"It's not the same as *having* her, though!" Hilary muttered to no one in particular.

But Miss Annersley was leaning forward on the desk, mischief in her face, and the girls were waiting eagerly to hear what more she had to say.

"I am sure you all want to know what we mean to do with you this time," she said gently, "but I'm afraid you must wait. We aren't telling you yet. I can assure you it will be something very good and quite fresh."

A groan came again at this tantalising statement, but it was hushed at once and she concluded.

"That is all for the moment. Tomorrow you will settle in to your forms and work will begin as usual on Monday. Stand!"

The school rose to its feet on the word.

"Turn!"

They all turned as Miss Annersley nodded to Miss Alton who swung round to the piano and struck a chord.

"March!"

Miss Alton began a lively march and the school stepped out smartly and dispersed, Juniors to bed and the rest to common-rooms or the trunk-room where they had to finish unpacking.

CHAPTER IV

TENNIS

NEXT morning, when the rest went off to their form-rooms to settle in and unpack their books, Katharine and the other new girls were taken to the Prefects' room and set down to test papers to decide which forms they should enter.

Dorothea Fletcher, Dilys Enderby and Norah Fitzgerald were twelve-year-olds; and Mary Hume informed the rest in one of the intervals that she was ten and had been sent to boarding-school because she was "a complete dud at lessons. Daddy says it's because I haven't a chance to do homework properly in a box of a house like ours. It's tiny —well, it's only a cottage, really. We've a kitchen-dining-room and a sitting-room and three bedrooms and the biggest isn't any larger than this. Daddy says we have to live on top of each other all the time. We've two boys younger'n me and we had a new baby at Christmas—she's *sweet*!—but it does make a crowd for us."

At this point, Miss Edwardes arrived with French papers, so Mary had to stop talking. Later, they were to find that whatever else she lacked, it was not conversational powers. Her own form complained bitterly that she talked "even on."

Norah Fitzgerald was from Galway and had been sent to school to be tamed. Her last exploit had been to take her father's newly purchased colt out and ride him bareback across the fields. It might have ended in a broken neck for her and broken knees for him, seeing that he was only half-trained. However, Norah's guardian angel had clearly been working overtime and the pair of them arrived in the stableyard unharmed, except for the shock to Diarmid's nerves.

Major Fitzgerald had been in the yard, too, and when she saw his face, Norah, as she freely owned, knew she had crowned her iniquities this time. Her immediate punishment had been a sound whipping, bed for a day, bread and water for a week and the loss of her own pony for the rest of the summer.

Then the Major decided that boarding-school was the only thing to tame his motherless girl, who had run wild far too long. Hence the arrival of Norah at the Chalet School. She was not, so far as anyone could see, particularly subdued and she openly expressed her intention of getting all the fun out of life that she could.

Dilys Enderby and Dorothea Fletcher were two rather prim young people who regarded the wild Norah with horror. They came from the same town, had attended the same small private school and evidently thought that life at the Chalet School would be much the same thing as at home. Katharine felt that they were due for more than one eye-opener.

In the afternoon she herself was summoned to the study, where Miss Wilson informed her that she was to try Upper Fourth, of which she would be the twenty-fifth member.

"Most of your subjects are well up to standard," "Bill," as the school called her—strictly behind her back for the most part—informed the new girl. "Pay a little more attention to spelling, please, Katharine; and remember that padding will gain you no marks here."

Katharine reddened. She had been called to order for these sins more than once before. However, "Bill" was always merciful with new girls, so she only told her to go and find her form, who were having French conversation at that period, and the girl escaped, thankful to be let off so lightly.

She heard later that Norah, Dorothea, and Dilys were all placed in Upper Third, though there had been some talk of trying Norah in Lower Fourth. However, they started her in the easier form for the first week or two. The chatty Mary Hume was placed in Upper Second.

Katharine found her form-room easily enough, for all the doors bore the form number. She tapped and was told to enter and found Mlle de Lachenais hard at it with the twenty-four girls who were sitting at their desks, all discussing—or trying to discuss—the latest film which most of them had seen during the holidays.

Mlle, a charming Frenchwoman who was, as saucy Jo Maynard once told her, one of the foundation stones of the school, having taught in it when even that lady had been a schoolgirl, welcomed the newcomer with a smile, told Hilary to find her a seat and asked if she spoke French at all.

"Mais oui, certainement, Mademoiselle," Katharine replied promptly.

French had no terrors for her since she had spent a good many holidays in France with Aunt Luce and had learned to chatter fluently as a result. She joined animatedly in the discussion about the film and Mlle was enchanted with her pretty accent as well as her fluency.

"I say," Hilary remarked in complete defiance to rules as they went to change into tennis shoes when the bell rang, "you *will* be Mlle's blue-eyed boy if you can keep *that* going. Where did you learn to gabble like that?"

Before Katharine could reply, a stern voice demanded, "Is that you talking, Hilary?"

"Ye-yes, Nita," Hilary stammered, turned red.

Nita, a small, slight girl of nearly eighteen, surveyed the culprit thoughtfully. "I should have thought you knew the rules by this time. If it happens next week, it'll mean a fine. Just you remember that and try to hold your tongue."

She said no more, but signed to them to march off, and Hilary was silent until they were outside when she explained to Katharine.

"That's Nita Eltringham, one of the prees. She runs the Hobbies Club. Rather a pet, really. I suppose I asked for trouble, yattering like that in the Splash."

"Are there a lot of prefects?" Katharine asked.

"Eight Seniors, including the Head Girl and the Games Prefect and three Juniors," Hilary responded. "If they want any more help, they call on Special Sixth."

"How's that—and who are Special Sixth?"

"They're the folk who have stayed on to specialise in one thing or another. They drop prefect work when they do that, but they'll hoe in when necessary. There never are very many of them—six this year. Here we are at the courts so we'd better not yatter any more. I'll tell you the rest later."

The courts on which the Middles played were situated at the far end of the big garden. There were four of them and three practice-stands at one side as well. Miss Burn, looking very trig and smart in her well-cut shorts and college blazer, was waiting for them and two prefects were chatting with her. Later on, Katharine was to learn that the prefects and some of the younger mistresses always helped with games as the forms were fairly large.

Miss Burns quickly made up three sets and sent them off to the courts to begin. Then she turned to Katharine.

"Have you played before?" she queried.

As it happened, Katharine had played from the time that she could get a ball over the net. Aunt Luce was a keen player and she had seen to it that her niece was well taught. In addition, tennis had been the summer game at Katharine's last school, though there they had played on hard courts.

She replied modestly that she had learned for five or six years and Miss Burn promptly called Madge Watson, Elinor Pennell and Blossom Willoughby and sent them with Katharine for a set on the remaining court. The rest she assigned to the practice-boards with big Dickie Christy in charge.

"Anyone else free but you and Judy?" she asked, before that young lady went to take duty. "What about— let me see—what are Peggy and Daphne doing?"

"Peggy's at extra German and Daph's in the library making notes for her history essay," Dickie replied.

"Oh? Anyone else free? No? Then run along to your lambs and I'll see if I can get someone from Special Sixth. Keep your eye on Armine Browne, by the way. You remember how she used to swipe last summer."

Dickie nodded and departed, and Miss Burn summoned one Barbara Walton and sent her to Special Sixth with a message which resulted in Anthea Barnett and a slight, foreign-looking girl joining them.

"Anthea, take Meg's set," Miss Burn ordered. "Natalie, you take on Gwen Parry's, will you? *Now* I think we're all right. Chosen your partners, you four? Toss for side, will you, Blossom?"

Blossom, one of the prettiest girls Katharine had ever seen, tossed and lost, so Madge and Katharine chose the side with their backs to the light, leaving Blossom and Elinor service.

Blossom took the first service and the pace of the ball she sent across the net made Katharine open her eyes. Madge just got to it, but she sent it very tamely into the other court where Elinor returned it to Katharine in a very easy lob. Katharine was waiting, and she smashed it

31

down with all her force. Blossom tried to get to it, but it beat her and the first point went to Katharine and Madge.

Blossom and Elinor changed sides and again the ball came furiously over. Katharine returned it to Elinor in a low, almost equally swift return. Elinor took, but again Katharine was at the net to smash it down and it fell dead.

"Love thirty!" Miss Burn called, her grey eyes eager.

Blossom glanced across at the new girl as she scooped up the balls. "I say! You *can* play! Have a singles with me one evening next week if we can bag a court, will you?"

Katharine nodded. "I'd love to!"

"Don't chatter, girls! Talk afterwards!" Miss Burn commanded. "Ready, Madge?"

Madge missed this time and the point went to the other pair; but Katharine's return to Blossom on the next service completely beat that young person; and Madge, on her mettle now, returned the final ball of the game with that most maddening of all returns—a gentle trickle over the net.

"Take service, Katharine," Miss Burn said. "I want to see what your service is like."

Katharine picked up the balls with an inward qualm. Aunt Luce had told her more than once that her service was far too erratic. At her best, it was almost untakeable with a nasty twist. At her worst, it could be an appalling skyer.

She tossed up the first ball and drove it firmly out of court. The second was an easy one that Blossom smashed into the far corner of the court, and quite out of reach. Madge and Katharine crossed over and Katharine was facing Elinor Pennell, who was merely a good average. This time, the new girl made no mistake. The ball was well in the court and it broke out so that Elinor missed it completely and the score stood at fifteen all.

By this time, Katharine had steadied and Blossom only just managed to return the next service. Katharine volleyed it back to Elinor, who drove to Madge. Madge returned it to the back line and Katharine, who was now at the net, sent it into the far corner where it broke in, beating the waiting Blossom utterly. She got it, but only sent it into the net.

As there were other people to play, the girls were restricted to seven games a set, so when four-three had been called in favour of Blossom and Elinor, they were sent to the practice-boards and another four took their places. While the new set were preparing, Miss Burn spoke to the four who had just played.

"Your pace is good, Blossom," she said, "but you need to place your balls more. Practise that, please. Madge, you simply *must not* dream on the court. Twice you missed easy balls because your mind was elsewhere. Watch that; it isn't fair on your partner. Elinor, you must put your back into your service. You can get more speed on it if you try. Katharine, your service *can* be very good, but you served some awful outsiders. You must learn to play evenly. Now go to the practice-boards."

She turned back to the court and the four strolled over to the practice-boards. Hilary, Meg, Hilda, and Gwen Parry, the form prefects, were all finishing a strenuous practice. Hilary gave the new girl a respectful look.

"I say, you *can* hit them up!" she said. "I saw you once or twice and I was jolly thankful I wasn't playing against you. You might show me how to manage that squiggly service of yours."

"Oh, rather!" Katharine said.

Blossom turned to them. "Can't we fix up a four for one night next week? You, Hilary, and Katharine, and—"

"Gwen Parry," interjected Madge swiftly. "She's a good player."

Gwen, a dark, Welsh girl with a pleasant face, grinned at Madge. "Thanks for the comp. I say, Katharine——"

"Cave! Burnie's got her eye on you," another girl interrupted. "She thinks you folk are doing too much yattering. Have a go at the practice-board, Katharine."

She stood back, yielding her place to the new girl, and Katharine picked up her racquet and dealt with the practice balls for ten minutes, intent on placing rather than pace.

Blossom was at another, doing the same thing. They gave it up to some of the rest presently and sat down with their blazers pulled round them to gossip quietly.

"D'you play cricket as well as you do tennis?" Hilary asked.

Katharine shook her head. "I've only played single stump when I was a kid. We didn't play it at my last school."

"Then there's a chance for some of us," the girl who

had given Katharine her place at the practice-board re-marked with a grin. "I wondered if you were an infant phenomenon there as well as at tennis. I say, Katharine, how do you get that break of yours? I was watching your set part of the time and it beat even Blossom."

"You're telling *me*!" Blossom spoke feelingly. "I simply must have a stab at it some time if you'll show me, Kath."

"I'll show anyone," Katharine replied amiably. "Aunt Luce taught me as soon as I could get a ball over the net from the back line. Blossom, you *are* swift! You've a service almost like a man's! "

"I've played such lots with Dad and Mother," Blossom explained. "Dad's awfully keen and so is Mother, only she won't have any time this summer. There've been just three of us for ages—my brother Toby and me and Judy, my kid sister who's in Upper Second and is just nine. Then, just before we broke up for Easter, we had another brother, and he's awfully delicate, so Mother won't be able to play this summer, she says. She'll have her hands full with Aubrey."

"Is that his name? It's a pretty one."

Blossom nodded. "Aubrey Julian after his two god-fathers. He's sweet, but very tiny and white." Her lovely face was very grave as she finished and the others hurried to change the subject.

"You'll learn cricket here, Kath," Hilda Jukes re-marked, using the abbreviation Blossom had provided. "If you're mad on it like Tom Gay and some of the others you can have three cricket practices and one tennis in the week. If you prefer tennis, it'll be the other way round."

Katharine looked thoughtful, though her heart was warm at that chummy "Kath." "I've never played as I told you. I expect I'll stick to tennis, though I'll be glad to know cricket too."

"Better wait to make up your mind until we see if you're an undiscovered cricket genius," Madge said with a grin.

"I'm certain I'm not," Katharine retorted firmly.

"You never can tell. Wait until they ask you to choose —which won't be for three weeks or so—and then see how you feel," Hilary told her as the bell rang for the end of tennis and they picked up their racquets and went to form into line to march back to the house.

CHAPTER V

THE MYSTERY TRUNK

"PLEASE, Miss Moore, may Katharine Gordon go to the study?"

Miss Moore stopped short in her lesson to Upper Fourth on seasonal and constant winds and turned to the Junior who had brought the message. She saw a tiny girl, since Verity-Anne Carey was very small for her age. She had long fair curls tied back from an oval face whose features were cut with the delicacy of a cameo. The gentian-blue eyes she had raised to those of the new geography mistress were full of a saintly expression that most of the old hands could have told Miss Moore was quite out of place.

Miss Moore, however, was new that term, very young and guileless, since her two terms out of college had been spent in having an operation for appendix trouble and convalescing from the same. She was greatly impressed by Verity-Anne's angel-child look. She smiled down into the small face as she said, "Certainly. Katharine Gordon?"

Katharine stood up. "Yes, Miss Moore?"

"You are wanted in the study. Go at once, please."

Katharine went to the door where she turned and bobbed the curtsy insisted on for manners by the school and one of the legacies of its continental origin. Then she left the geography-room, accompanied by Verity-Anne, whom she knew to be one of Mary-Lou's greatest pals.

"I think it's your trunk," said that young person in her tiny silvery voice.

"Do you mean it's come? Oh, thank goodness for that!"

It was well into the middle of the week and so far nothing had been heard of her trunk. Matron had made herself very unpleasant to the railway officials when Tuesday arrived and no trunk had turned up. Now, on Thursday, her unpleasantness would seem to have justified itself.

Katharine parted from Verity-Anne at the door of

Upper Third and scurried on to the study where she found Miss Annersley and Matron awaiting her.

"Come in, Katharine," the former said. "Now tell me, how many trunks did your aunt send you?"

Katharine stood stock-still. "Only one, Miss Annersley."

"Are you *sure*?"

Katharine pondered before she answered that one. So far as she knew, only one had been sent. Unfortunately, you never knew what Aunt Luce might take it into her head to do. *Could* she have suddenly decided that her niece might need more than had already been provided? It would be quite like her!

"I only helped to pack one," she said finally.

"Well, two have arrived," Matron informed her. "Both are addressed to 'Gordon,' though one has only 'Chalet School, South Wales' on the label. The other is fully addressed."

Katharine was dumbfounded—not at being told of the scant address. That, again, was just like Aunt Luce. But that she could have labelled the other correctly seemed too good to be true, since the Head's letter had most certainly been lost. It was only by good luck that either of them had remembered her name to be Wilson, for Aunt Luce had made all arrangements herself in the end, and only told her niece later.

Miss Annersley saw her bewildered look.

"Perhaps the best thing will be to go through the trunks," she said. "Not now, of course. You mustn't miss your work. What are you doing this afternoon?"

Katharine considered. "Needlework from two till three and then art till half-past four," she said.

"Then it will be quite easy. When the two o'clock bell rings, go to the trunk-room and we'll unpack the trunks. Then you won't miss art," the Head said. Then she added with a smile, "I expect you will be very glad to have a proper change."

"Oh, I shall!" Katharine spoke in heartfelt tones.

It was all very well during the day when it was still not warm enough for summer frocks. Tunic and blazer were produced by the school together with the various badges; but when the others had changed into velveteen evening frocks, she had had to be content with a skirt and blouse.

Miss Annersley understood. "You'll be able to change properly tonight," she said with a smile. "Very well. Run along back to your work now. I'll explain to Mlle about the needlework."

"Thank you," Katharine said. She made her curtsy and escaped.

When she had gone, Matron and the Head laughed together.

"I suppose that's what comes of having an artist for a guardian," Miss Annersley remarked. She suddenly looked thoughtful. "You know, Matey, I really had no idea until she told us that she was any relation of Lucia Gordon's."

"Well, I suppose her mother or whoever made the arrangements didn't think it necessary to say anything about that," Matron replied.

"It was her father's lawyer. her parents are abroad and she came to us from a prep school near London."

"Oh, well, I don't suppose any lawyer would worry much about an artist," Matron said as she rose to go back to her work. "I'm thankful her trunk—or trunks —are here at last. We've managed; but it hasn't been too easy."

She departed and Miss Annersley turned to answer the telephone which rang at that moment. It was a trans-Atlantic call, and in the excitement of hearing that the Maynard family had reached Toronto safely and all was well with the entire family, she forgot Katharine completely.

When the bell rang for afternoon school, Katharine, duly primed by the rest of her form, went to Mlle Berné who took their needlework—and, incidentally, made it an occasion for improving their French conversation—and asked to be excused.

"But why should I?" she had demanded when the rest had assured her that she must go. "The Head *said* she'd explain."

"That doesn't matter. It's decent manners, and they put every farthing of twopence on good manners in this establishment," Hilary maintained.

Mlle gave smiling consent and Katharine, only pausing long enough to see that she was tidy, went flying up the back stairs, two at a time, and along to the trunk-room where Matron was waiting for her.

37

"Well, here you are," that lady said, pointing to the two trunks standing side by side in the middle of the floor.

Katharine looked at them. They were exactly alike and the labels had been printed in neat block letters so there was nothing to be learned from their exteriors.

"Give me your keys and we'll open them," Matron said.

Warned by the others, Katharine had secured her keys before Mittagessen, as lunch was called by the school. She produced them and Matron speedily had the trunks unlocked, though the key turned very stiffly and reluctantly in one. The lids were thrown back and Katharine looked in.

"This is the one I helped to pack," she said, touching the first. "I don't know a thing about the other."

Matron picked up a typewritten sheet that lay on top of the stranger.

" 'Name-tapes not yet arrived. Will forward later'," she read. "Well, take one of those baskets and begin to put your things in. Wait; you need some help. You'd better go and ask Mlle to excuse someone. Hurry, now! There's no time to waste! "

Katharine sped off to ask if Hilary might be excused and the pair came racing back, Hilary only too pleased to be excused from her loathed sewing.

They unpacked Katharine's own venture first. She recognised all her things—the pretty underwear and simple frocks Aunt Luce had helped her choose; the smartly-cut coat and the big white hat packed at the bottom in Aunt Luce's patent way which kept the hat firmly in place and the brim supported by rolled stockings under it, while the crown was filled with handkerchiefs; the shoes and slippers; all her own little personal possessions, including some Malayan carvings in ivory and the family of little wooden bears Aunt Luce had once brought her from Berne.

It was when this one was emptied and pushed to one side that the girls began to feel excited. Katharine simply could not understand a second supply of garments. Neither could she make head or tail of the message about name-tapes. If there *was* one thing in all this muddle of which she could be certain, it was that she had none. Aunt Luce had declared that so long as everything was marked clearly, that was all that mattered. Her niece had spent hours sitting printing her name on everything, and used up two bottles of marking-ink in the process!

Matron was waiting. Hilary set the long, light wicker tray down beside the trunk and Katharine began to lift out the contents while Matron checked them off on the enclosed list.

The first thing to appear was another big white hat. Beneath it was a parcel which Katharine undid to find herself staring at a gaudy handkerchief sachet of green satin, pen-painted with scarlet poppies and wheatears. It contained a dozen handkerchiefs of finest coloured linen, all marked with the monogram K.M.G.—or M.K.G. as you chose to read it.

Katharine handed the thing to Hilary in startled silence and took out some sets of crêpe-de-chine underclothes of a kind she had never worn in her life.

"Aunt Luce must be ravers!" was the only thought in her mind as she handed them over.

Frocks followed, one of Swiss muslin, a blue in some silky material, a yellow one beautifully embroidered with sprays of green leaves. All were quite as simple as her own, but the quality was another thing altogether.

"That makes two evening frocks too many," Matron informed her. "There were three in the other trunk. You may choose which you'll have and the other two can be packed away for the holidays."

Katharine regarded them with staring eyes. "I—I simply don't understand this," she said. "I don't think I want any of them, thank you, Matron. I have enough with the others."

"Your aunt evidently doesn't think so," Matron retorted. "You had better keep the muslin and I'll pack the other two away. Here you are F lary. Handle it carefully. They're beautifully packed and quite uncreased."

The usual schoolgirl belongings followed, all of super-fine quality, but all quite girlish and in good taste. All the same, Katharine was speedily becoming convinced that Aunt Luce really must have taken leave of her senses this time, when the climax was reached as she took out some sheets and there, under everything else, lay an enormous teddy-bear.

Katharine's mind was made up at sight of this. However mad Aunt Luce might be, she would never include such a thing in a schoolgirl's trunk. She hauled the creature out and stood up, clutching it.

"Please, Matron," she said, "I'm certain there's some mistake. This isn't my trunk—*can't* be! I haven't had a teddy since I was a—a small child in Samoa. I don't even know what became of him. I never saw him after we left. I expect he got left behind or was given to someone."

Matron looked at the trunk and then at the bear. It was quite clear that he was no new thing. He was scrupulously clean, but had either been washed or dry-cleaned recently. Part of his fur had been worn away in places and one eye had been set in askew, giving him a squint. The three people regarding him all felt that whoever owned him loved him dearly.

Hilary stooped to twist round the label tied to one of the handles of the trunk and read it.

"It *says* 'Gordon'," she said doubtfully. "We haven't another Gordon in the school—unless it's one of the Kinders—Oh, but it couldn't be! Those aren't frocks for a Kinder.

Matron closed down the lid and surveyed the label stuck thereon. There could be no doubt about it. The trunk was addressed to "Gordon" clearly enough.

She looked again at Katharine, but the girl's expression was transparently bewildered. Matron had spent the best of her life at the Chalet School. She knew girls inside out and was far too old a campaigner to be easily taken in by anyone. Katharine was definitely not "trying it on." She was quite as puzzled as anyone else.

Matron's gaze fell to Katharine's feet and her face cleared. The shoes and slippers from the second trunk were for a short broad foot, and the new girl had a long slender one. Matron doubted if she could even attempt to wear any of the second supply of footgear.

"Sit down and try these on," she ordered, handing her a pair of shoes.

Katharine sat down, pulled off her own house-slippers and tried to do as she was told. As Matron had foreseen, her foot slipped up to the toe of the new pair easily enough, but the heel was at least half-an-inch too short.

"Yes; you're right," Matron said thoughtfully. "Those shoes won't go near you—for length. Or could your aunt have forgotten your size?" she added with a sudden afterthought.

"She couldn't possibly," Katharine replied. "We take the same size. These are miles too wide for me and not nearly long enough. If they were, I'd slop about all over the place if I tried to walk in them."

"Better English, if you please!" Matron snapped at her. "Well, it's plain there has been some queer mistake. I'd better see Miss Annersley or Miss Wilson about it. In the meantime, you can put that creature back into the trunk and all the rest of the things, too. Leave the dresses and coats to me, though. They must be carefully packed since they obviously belong to someone else."

"Oh, Matron!" Hilary had been nearly bursting with it for the last two minutes and could contain herself no longer. "Do you think it should have gone to the Chalet School at Tanswick?"

"No, I do not!" Matron retorted. "The thing's addressed clearly enough to St Briavel's. There's no mistake there."

She pointed to the labels and the mystified girls bent to read them.

"Well, I just don't understand it," Hilary said with finality. She giggled. " 'The Mystery of the Unknown Trunk'—sounds like a new thriller!"

"Don't talk nonsense!" Matron told her austerely.

An awful thought had come to Katharine. There certainly *had* been a mistake. Could it possibly be Aunt Luce's? Had she really been entered for the Tanswick Chalet School instead of here and was that where she ought to have been all this time?

What a simply ghastly thing if it were really so! And how on earth could they ever find out? It would be no use writing to Aunt Luce, for no one could say just whereabouts on the continent of Europe that lady might be. She had *said* Lourdes, and mentioned Andorra to follow; but that didn't mean that she would stick to it. *Here* was a pretty mess!

And then Hilary put the coping-stone to the whole affair. She had consoled herself for "Matey's" last snub by stooping to look at the labels on Katharine's own trunk. Now she stood upright to ejaculate, "Your own trunk just says 'South Wales.' Oh, Katharine, do you think your Aunt could possibly have been meaning you to go to the Chalet School at Tanswick? And if she did, where on earth is the *other* Katharine Gordon?"

41

CHAPTER VI

THE MYSTERY THICKENS

MISS ANNERSLEY, when told the story, promptly rang up the school at Tanswick to explain matters, only to be told by a very assured young voice that they had their full complement of pupils and the only Gordon there was one Meta Gordon who had been at the school for the past three years. They knew nothing of any Katharine Mary Gordon. No; she was sorry, but Miss Wilson their Principal was not available, having been whisked off to Birmingham for a major operation. She was still seriously ill, and there could be no question of her being troubled by business matters for at least another six weeks.

This having got them no further forward, Miss Annersley next sent for her own secretary, Rosalie Dene, an old girl of the school and of the same vintage as Jo Maynard. She came into the room in her usual quiet way and the Head congratulated herself on having a secretary so very different from the Tanswick lady.

Miss Dene learned what was required, searched the files and found the card which held particulars. Mary Katharine Gordon was the daughter of Dr John Gordon of Singapore and she was fourteen and had been educated at a private school.

"I remember," Miss Dene said after nibbling the end of her pencil for a minute or so, "that we *said* the details were rather on the meagre side, but we could get anything else from the girl herself when she came. I meant to send for you before, Katharine, but there's been such a rush I forgot all about it. *Is* your father in Singapore?"

"He *was*. Then he got the appointment to the big hospital at Lan-po and Mother went with him—she's a trained nurse, you see."

The elders exchanged a quick glance but said nothing. Like Elinor Pennell, they had heard about the Chinese Government's action and knew that the fate of the Gordons at Lan-po was a mystery at the moment.

Miss Annersley finally decided to write to Miss Gordon through her bank and see what she could tell them. Until then, the only thing to do was to repack the strange trunk and put it away. Katharine had all she needed in any case.

By this time, the three o'clock bell had rung, so the Head sent the girls off to art after forbidding them to discuss the episode with anyone. She gave them an excuse note for Herr Laubach, the art master, and told Katharine to go to the office after tea and give Miss Dene the rest of her particulars.

"We must wait until we can get into touch with Miss Gordon," she told Matron and Miss Dene when the girls had departed.

"*Someone* seems to have muddled things finely!" was Matron's comment.

"Miss Gordon may be partly responsible for that—she's an artist and seems to be one of the kind who get wrapped up in what they are doing and let everything else go hang," the Head said. "What I really want to know, however, is where the other girl is. Obviously she exists, since her trunk has arrived. That being the case, I'm rather bothered about her."

Matron turned to Rosalie Dene. "Haven't you the letter that came when she was entered, Rosalie?" she asked.

Rosalie considered. Then light came. "Oh, Matey—don't you remember the flood? A whole pile of letters were lying on my desk while we three had our farewell tea with Jo. One of the taps in the bathroom overhead suddenly gave out and the bath overflowed and brought the ceiling down. We couldn't read most of those letters when they were finally rescued and they were burnt. I'm awfully afraid the Gordon letters were among them. I seem to remember something about it."

"They were," Miss Annersley nodded. "Bill had had them for reference and she took them back to your office before we set off for Jo's and dropped them in the 'Unanswered' basket. Then that tap went and we had the flood and the ceiling collapsed. Only the maids were in the house at the time, you may remember, and no one knew anything about it until Megan went to the office to ring up Evans at Carnbach about the daily papers and saw the mess."

She began to laugh and the other two joined in at the memory of that exciting event.

Rosalie took up the tale. "Never shall I forget what the office looked like when we returned at eight o'clock that night! Megan had found someone to turn off the water at the main; and she and the maids had mopped up what they could. But no one could do much about the plaster, and when the men came across next day and cleared up the mess most of those letters were sodden and fit only for the incinerator!"

"Well, this present business is beyond me," Matron remarked as she stood up and pushed her chair back against the wall. "As for the other girl, you needn't worry about her. You'd have had whoever is in charge of her down on you long before this if they hadn't known all about her. You write to Miss Gordon, Hilda, and see what she has to say. In the meantime, I'd see Katharine and Hilary again and impress it on them that they are to say nothing until you give them permission. We don't want any shilling shockers running round the school!"

On this note she departed and the two left behind looked at each other again and laughed.

"When it comes to a little sound common sense, commend me to Matey!" the Head said with a final chuckle.

Miss Dene rose to go, for she was very busy. "This *is* a place for happenings, isn't it? Last term Carola Johnstone gate-crashed us and caused any amount of trouble. Last year it was that little ass, Annis Lovell who gave us all such a nasty shock. And when *I* was a mere pupil, there was always Jo to keep us from being bored."

Miss Annersley laughed again. "There always *is* Jo," she retorted. "However, for once in a way she *can't* have any finger in the pie. That will be something new for her. By the way, Rosalie, you might try and get the Mordaunts on the 'phone for me later on. Edgar Mordaunt might know something about the Gordons. One of his pals works at the Foreign Office and if he doesn't know anything himself, I expect he could pull a few strings and find out if they have any further news from Lan-po."

Miss Dene nodded and went off to tackle some of the school's piles of correspondence while the Head, resolutely putting the latest mystery out of her head for the time being, turned to her correcting and the Sixth Form's essays on "Journeying through Britain."

As for Katharine and Hilary, they flew to the art-room where Herr Laubach, head of the art staff, awaited them. He accepted their explanation that they were so late because they had been with the Head only after he had read that lady's note. Then he grunted and sent them to their seats after he had demanded Katharine's name and told them to work hard in order to make up for lost time and not chatter.

All this being in German, Katharine was not much wiser. Hilary explained in an undertone before she settled down to do her best with the upturned pudding-basin set on a pastry-board against a background of tea-towel with a couple of crossed spoons laid negligently to one side that was the afternoon's group.

Herr Laubach, having seen them begun, went to the other side of the room to Gwen Parry who was getting into difficulties. Promptly a volley of eager questions was hissed at the pair from all sides.

"Miss Annersley wanted us," was all Hilary would say and Katharine only shook her head.

Nor could either be coaxed into being any more definite, though Upper Fourth did their best. Finally, Herr Laubach finished with Gwen and came back to see what the opposite end of his class was doing, so talking had to cease perforce.

He bent over Katharine's effort and his bushy brows met in a mighty frown as he demanded, "Vat ees dis?"

Katharine went scarlet and said nothing. Drawing was no gift of hers, and while her basin might have been a good-sized pintray, her spoons, in proportion, should have been garden spades, though of a new and original shape.

"Now," said Herr Laubach pushing her gently from her seat and sitting down himself, "I vill you show how zee correct proportions ve make—shut zee eye and hold zee pencil like zo, and zo. Zen ve see zat zee bowl he is larger zan ze spoons. Now you try him and I vill kom back later."

He unpinned the spoilt sheet from her drawing-board, crumpled it up and threw it into the waste-paper basket, gave her a fresh sheet and left her to try again while he went to Jennifer Penrose, who had finished her outlines and wanted to know if she might begin shading.

Katharine sat down again and proceeded to imitate his action with the pencil—with additions of her own. She shut one eye as he had told her. Then she screwed up her mouth, sucked her cheeks in and, in her tense concentration, *wobbled her nose like a rabbit*!

Hilda Jukes happened to glance up in time to get the full beauty of this grimace and collapsed in helpless giggles which she tried vainly to smother. Louder and louder became her titters and, unfortunately, the girls round about were infected and began tittering, too, without the faintest idea as to what the joke was.

Herr Laubach, having finished with Jennifer, looked up. By this time, Katharine had stopped making faces and was still regarding the others with a startled air, wondering in all innocence why they were giggling so madly.

It had only needed this to complete Hilda's disruption. She was a giggler at the best of times and had begun the afternoon in a more than usually risible condition. Now, as she caught Katharine's amazed stare, she gave up all attempt at self-control and burst into shrieks of laughter. The rest followed her example and, despite a thunderous-looking Herr Laubach, the art-room rang with their mirth.

Herr Laubach was possessed of a hair-trigger temper, as Jo Maynard could have told anyone. He loved his art and was all too often sorely tried by the efforts of the girls. On this occasion he realised that Hilda, who was rapidly growing hysterical, was the root cause of the disturbance and did what was, perhaps, the only thing that would put a stop to it all. With a bound which sent two desks spinning he was before her, had seized her by the shoulders and was shaking her.

Hilda had reached the stage where she was red, tearful, and actually crowing. She had not expected his onslaught and his treatment made her bite her tongue smartly. All desire to laugh left her as the pain brought fresh tears to her eyes, and the rest, startled out of their silly infection, suddenly fell silent.

Meanwhile, Herr Laubach was demanding, "Vat ees zee meaning of zis? I you vill to Mees Vilson and Miss Annersley report. Vy 'ave you laugh like zis?"

"I—I——" stammered Hilda; but got no further.

"You von bad girl are!" Herr Laubach stormed at her. "From zis room go—*go*, I say!" with a stamp of his foot.

Only too thankful to get away, Hilda fled in confusion, the rest fell to work immediately, and the rest of the lesson was continued in deadly silence.

As for Hilda, she had sought refuge in the splashery, where she wiped away the tears of pain and then sat down behind the stand, well out of sight of the doorway in case anyone should glance in. From time to time she began to giggle again as she recalled that appalling grimace of Katharine's, but her sore tongue kept her within bounds. Besides she knew very well that she would get no marks for the afternoon's work and if Miss Slater, their form mistress, noticed it and asked questions, *then*, to quote Hilda's reflections, the fat *would* be in the fire!

Once she had thought it over, the girl did Katharine the justice to realise that the whole thing had been unintentional on her part. Unfortunately, the recollection of the latter's astounded face made her giggle again and the sound attracted the attention of Peggy Bettany who happened to be passing.

Peggy opened the door wider and peeped in. She could see no one, but the giggles came from the far side of the room. The Head Girl came in, shut the door behind her, stalked round the end of the stand and saw, as she had begun to suspect, Hilda Jukes sitting on top of a shoe-locker and literally writhing with merriment.

Peggy was slight and dainty, very pretty and gentle as a rule; but no one could better her discipline when she chose.

"Hilda Jukes!" she exclaimed in her sternest tones. "What do you think you are doing?"

Hilda came to her senses in a hurry. "Herr Laubach sent me out of art," she said meekly, rising to her feet as she spoke.

Peggy eyed her slowly and steadily from head to foot and back again and Hilda stared at the ground and felt herself growing scarlet.

"In-deed?" Peggy's tone was icy. "Why, may I ask?"

"I—I laughed."

"Oh? You laughed?"

A silence followed, during which Hilda wished the floor would open and swallow her. Meanwhile, Peggy continued that chilly gaze and it was not until she felt that her victim was properly subdued that she condescended to speak again.

"Why?" she asked.

Hilda was in a quandary. She would not tell tales, but she knew from past experience that Peggy meant to have an answer.

"It—it was something I—I saw," she said at last.

"What was it?"

No reply.

"What was it?" Peggy repeated inexorably.

Still no reply. Peggy laid down the armful of books which she had gone to the library to bring, and settled herself comfortably on a locker.

"Get this, Hilda," she said steadily. "You don't stir from this place until you answer me. What was it you were laughing at?"

It was an impasse. Hilda was not going to say that Katharine had been making faces, but neither could she think of any way of getting out of it that Peggy was likely to accept. Having said that she meant to have an answer, Peggy knew better than to back down, so the pair stayed where they were in silence. Hilda, wildly revolving in her mind all sorts of ideas, could find nothing that would meet the case. Luckily for both, the bell rang for the end of school. Peggy stood up.

"Go and change," she said in chilling tones. "I will see you in the prefects' room after tea."

She left the splashery without waiting to see whether Hilda did or did not obey her and that young lady decided to wait for the rest and go up with them in case Matron met her and wanted to know why she was so much earlier than the others.

Upper Fourth came marching along in a minute or so and as soon as they were safely in the splashery, their tongues were loosed although, as it was a "French" day which meant that all conversation must be in French, they were not quite as fluent as they might have been. All the same, thanks to the deadly silence of last half-hour, they had quite a good deal prepared.

"Hilda Jukes!" Gwen Parry exclaimed. "Pourquoi avez-vous vous moquée?"

"Herr Laubach était—er—furieuse," Jennifer added.

"He's—I mean, il est masculin," Meg Whyte giggled.

"Oh, well—I mean, eh bien!" Jennifer shrugged.

"Oh, ça ne fait rien!" This was a well-known remark with Upper Fourth who made it serve a good many purposes. "Taisez-vous toutes!" Gwen ordered. "Hilda, pourquoi avez-vous vous moquée?"

"J'ai seen—er—vu une personne grimacer," Hilda replied. Her French was not much better than her art.

"Si vous voulez dire 'make a face," il faut dire 'faire une grimace'," Hilary told her with a superior air. "Qui a fait une grimace?"

"Personne!" Hilda retorted. She knew that one, having had to write out twenty-five times in her best hand-writing: " 'No one' in French is 'personne'."

Elinor Pennell grinned. "Je l'ai vu aussi," she said. "Je suis sûre qu'elle n'avait pas l'intention de—de faire cela."

"Qui est-ce?" half a dozen voices demanded.

"Katharine," Elinor told them.

"*Me!*" Katharine sounded stunned.

Hilda with a sigh of relief nodded. "Oui: c'était vous."

"But—but——"

"Parlez en français, Katharine," Hilary said briskly. "You've got to, sooner or later. Anyhow you can—I mean," she added lamely, "Vous le pouvez."

Katharine nodded. "Merci bien. Hilda, quand est-ce que j'ai fait une grimace?"

"Quand Herr Laubach a montrê à vous comme vous—" Hilda broke down here and finished in English. "How you measure for proportions.

Katharine looked thunderstruck. "Mais je vous assure—" she began; but Elinor struck in again.

"Déjà j'ai dit qu j'en suis sûre. C'était une grimace involontaire."

"C'était une grimace—what's the French for 'ghastly' someone? 'Effrayeuse'?—merci beaucoup." Hilda spoke with conviction. "Vous avez—French for 'wobbled,' please—Oh, vous faisiez trembler le nez."

"I did *what*?" Katharine forgot again and dropped into English.

"Wobbled your nose—like a rabbit," Hilda said in desperation. "Comme un lapin," she added to make it absolutely clear.

Katharine stared at her, wide-eyed for a moment. Then she went as red as ever Hilda had done, and exclaimed, "*Oh!* What a triple *ass* I am!" in tones of such self-reproach that the rest eyed her amazedly.

"It is a foolish habit of mine," she told them in French

—and very shamefacedly. "I have been scolded for doing it and I thought I had cured myself. I suppose I did it because Herr Laubach upset me. I am so sorry, Hilda. I will go at once and explain to him that it was my fault you laughed."

"Oh, no you won't!" Hilda cried. "I mean, vous ne faisiez pas cela. C'est fini—so far as *he's* concerned, anyhow," she added in English.

"Alors—" Katharine began.

Gwen Parry got there before her. "Qui est-ce? Mlle Wilson?"

Hilda shook her head. "Peggy Bettany."

"Qu'avez-vous dit?" a chorus demanded.

"Rien, of course!"

"Et Peggy?" Hilda asked.

Hilda reddened again. "Peggy est très angry."

"Qu'est-ce qu'elle a dit?" Katharine asked.

"Oh, ça est facile," Meg Whyte said airily. "Hilda faut aller à Peggy après le feefe-o'clock." This last being the girls' expression in French for tea.

"Est-ce que c'est vrai?" Katharine turned to Hilda, who nodded reluctantly.

"Eh bien, j'y vais moi-même."

"There's no need. It wasn't your fault! I was born a giggler and I can't help it! Elinor saw you and *she* didn't giggle. She's not one—lucky her!" By this time, even her English seemed to be deserting Hilda. "You're not to go!"

"Hilda! En français, s'il vous plaît!" Gwen cried.

Hilda only shrugged her shoulders.

"Pourquoi êtes-vous ici? Dépêchez-vous, montez l'escalier," remarked the voice of Dickie Christy with a good British accent. "Allez-vous-en!"

They scuttled off with the argument left unfinished. Nor was there time to reopen it upstairs. They had wasted so much time in the splashery that they had left themselves very little time for changing. As it was, they managed to join the tea-parade only by the skin of their teeth.

The result was that when a tap sounded on the door of the prefects'. room after tea, two people entered in answer to Peggy's curt, "Entrez!" and that young lady found herself confronted by a determined Katharine who explained in fluent French that it was really *her* fault that Hilda had been caught giggling.

Peggy demanded the reason for this statement and, to

an audience of fascinated prefects, Katharine replied, "J'ai fait une grimace involontaire—comme ça!" and followed it up by a perfect imitation of a rabbit which made most of them promptly choke.

Peggy administered a brief rebuke on the folly of making faces—involontaires or otherwise—and advised Hilda to try to control herself better in future and let them go—only just in time to save most of her friends from suffocation through suppressed laughter.

The two Middles fled to find their books for preparation and had just settled down when Katharine, busily jotting down ideas for an essay on "Gardens," was sent for by Miss Annersley.

Arrived in the study, she found there both Miss Annersley and Miss Wilson with news for her. A letter had arrived from a Mr Matthieson, a London solicitor, in which he regretted that, owing to unforeseen circumstances, his ward, Mary Katharine Gordon, had not yet arrived at the school. She was with her mother in America where that lady, a musical comedy actress, was playing the lead in a new Musical and would not be coming before half-term, and possibly not till September.

"And now, Katharine," Miss Annersley said as she laid down the letter when she had read aloud such portions of it as she thought Katharine should hear, "we must find out exactly where you are supposed to be at school. It certainly is not here. Which is your aunt's bank? For I feel we must get into touch with her as soon as possible."

Katharine gave the desired information. Then she asked rather blankly, "Please, Miss Annersley, if I'm not supposed to be here and Tanswick says I'm not entered there, what am I to do?"

"Stay here until we do find out where you ought 'to be," Miss Wilson said crisply. "Judging by all *I* can hear, that is likely to be until half-term and after. So don't look so down in the mouth. You may yet remain with us. Funnier things than that have happened in my experience—especially of this school."

CHAPTER VII

LETTER FROM CANADA

THE post was late—"As usual!" Peggy Bettany said.
School was already in full swing when Bride
Bettany, prefect of Upper Fifth, which was the only
form to have windows looking out on the front lawns,
spied Lewis Griffiths lumbering up the drive. Upper Fifth
were very grown-up damsels in their own estimation, so
Bride most properly gave no hint of what she had seen
until Miss O'Ryan had gathered up her books and departed, leaving them to a period dedicated to French
essay.

When the door had closed behind the young mistress
and her retreating footsteps had died away, Bride glanced
round the remaining sixteen members of the form who
were opening dictionaries and French grammars, heading
their paper and otherwise preparing for three-quarters of
an hour's hard work, and said negligently, "Post came ten
minutes ago."

"He *would*!" Primrose Day finished filling her fountain
pen. "Why come at all, I sometimes wonder. Well, he's
no use to us until Break. You stop tantalising us, young
Bride, and give the thing you call your brain to French
essay. 'Le Siècle Passé'? Dear me! What on earth does
Mlle imagine that I, for one, can find to say about le
Siècle Passé?"

"That's what she's trying to find out," boyish Tom
Gay broke in. "For goodness' sake stop yattering and let
other folk do some work, even if you don't want to yourself. You're a nice one to talk to Bride!"

Primrose made a face at her, but as her cropped, wavy
head was already bent over her work again, it was wasted.
Miss Day heaved a sigh, wrote the title of the essay
neatly at the head of her sheet and set to work.

Meanwhile, in the study the Heads, who both had a
free period at this time, were sorting out the piles of
letters with Miss Dene in attendance.

"Those are for the Seniors, Rosalie," Miss Annersley
said at last. "These are for the Middles and this pile be-

longs to the Juniors. Is it Vi Lucy's birthday, by the way? She has five, I see."

"I believe it is. I know it's somewhere about this time."

"Find out from Miss Norman, will you? I can't think why Julie hasn't come to me if it is."

"I'll ask her," Miss Dene agreed. "Are those *our* letters?"

"Yes; you can take them to the staff-room when you go up for Break. *But*," Miss Annersley spoke impressively, "I have something very nice here and, unless I miss my guess, you are coming straight back to hear it."

"Letter from Jo!" Rosalie Dene spoke without hesitation as she scooped up the various piles of lettters and made for the door. "Wait till I come back—do! Don't skim *all* the cream before I come back!"

"We won't, I promise," the Head said, laughing as her secretary raced off to distribute her bundles. "Heavens! I know Jo has the pen of a ready writer, but she must have spent hours to accomplish all this!"

"Most likely she's collected all the family correspondence and sent it under one cover," Miss Wilson replied. "Open it and see. Yes; I thought so!" as the very big envelope was emptied and a variety of envelopes fluttered to the desk. "Let's sort them. Good gracious! Why has Jo seen fit to tie up her own budget?"

"Probably had an afterthought and had to break the seal of the envelope with no more handy—I know Jo!" Miss Annersley said as she struggled with the knot.

"Hurry up! What an age you take to undo a simple little reef-knot!"

"Well, a reef-knot may have been what Jo was aiming at, but she's certainly missed the bus this time." Miss Annersley was searching in a drawer as she spoke and produced a knife with which she cut the string. She opened the envelope and drew out several sheets, closely covered with the pretty writing which belonged to Jo Maynard, sister of Lady Russell, the owner of the school, old-time pupil and Head Girl when it was in Tirol, and now and always one of its moving spirits.

Jo had accompanied her husband to Canada where he was to attend an important medical conference and whither the Russells with their own two youngest girls and the third of Jo's triplet daughters, had gone the year before. Besides the five children left her in England, Jo had also taken Lady Russell's eldest girl, Sybil, and from all accounts would not be home again for some months.

The school at large missed her greatly. Jo's schoolday exploits had become almost legendary, for she had never been one of the tranquil kind, and added years, a long family, and a growing reputation as a writer for girls had done nothing to tone her down. This was the first real budget from her since she landed, so the Heads were anxious to know what she had been doing.

Miss Dene returned bringing Matey with her. Everyone knew that Jo was Matey's darling, so the secretary had torn breathlessly upstairs to fetch her to the study, so that she could share the feast, too.

"Oh, good!" Miss Annersley said as they entered the room. "The rest can hear Jo's novelette later. She's enclosed notes for a good many folk, anyway. Here are yours, you two. Don't bother with them now, though. We have just time to run through this before Break, I think, if you'll all sit quiet and refrain from interrupting."

They found seats for themselves and when they were settled, Miss Annersley, who had skimmed the letter quickly, began to read in the beautiful voice which was one of her greatest assets:

"My dear Hilda and Nell—and anyone else who's listening,

"First of all, we had a marvellous crossing. No one was sick and Charles lost the remains of his bad cold, for which I was duly grateful. I was also very thankful when I remembered that Jack had flown across and would be at St John's to meet us. I always did hate having to deal with the Customs on my own!

"By the way, I must also say that I've been more than glad that I listened to you two and took Rosa with us. However I should have managed without her I simply don't know. The girls were good enough, though Con was in a dream half the time as usual. I'm very much afraid my second girl is a born mooner! Len kept an eye on her, however, and Sybil weighed in when necessary.

"The real worries were Stephen and Michael. Steve contrived to pal up with one of the engineers—I haven't found out yet *which* one—and was for ever off with him. He was always filthy when he returned to me and I seriously wondered at one point how on earth I was to manage a set of decent clothes for him to land in.

"Mike, as you know, is one person's job, now he has found his feet. One moment he's close at hand, playing as good as gold. But take your eyes off him for one second and when you look again, he's vanished! I've never yet met anyone who could say definitely where he was likely to be found next, either!

"On one occasion, he landed up on the captain's bridge and when Rosa and I had exhausted pretty well everywhere we could think of, we heard that bubbly chuckle of his, falling from a blue sky, and looked up and there he was! The captain, I may add, was highly amused at him. He advised me in all seriousness to send him into the service as soon as he was old enough as he was clearly born to be a sailor.

"After that particular performance, Rosa nearly tied him to herself unless he was asleep, so we had no more real trouble that way, though I shudder to think how *I* should have ended up if I'd had him on my own—straws in the hair, I should imagine.

"Charles was the least bother of the lot. He was still rather pulled down by his cold when we sailed and preferred to cuddle up beside me and listen to almost endless stories. Thank goodness the last remnants vanished by the time we landed!

"When we *did* reach St John's, I was bitterly disappointed to be met by only Jack. As husbands go, he isn't a bad propositon; but I *had* expected to see Jem and the girls, if no one else. I'm sure my face fell a yard.

" 'Where's the others?' I demanded.

" 'In Toronto,' says Jack blandly.

"Toronto?' I shrieked. 'Why aren't they *here?* Perhaps Madge couldn't manage it with six-month-old babies; but there was nothing to prevent Jem coming and bringing my Margot, anyhow.'

"Jack patted me—the wretch! He knows I hate it!— and said, 'Now, keep calm, do. You'll see her all in good time. Jem has three important meetings this week so he couldn't get away; and I don't suppose you expected him to put that imp of ours on the train and send her alone to welcome us?'

"Well, I didn't. All the same, it was a drop.

" 'Another two days!' I mourned.

" 'Keep cool; it won't be even one day.'

" 'What do you mean?' says I haughtily.

" 'We're flying, lovey.'

"I nearly fell through the deck. *'Flying?'*

" 'Everyone flies over here, and I didn't exactly fancy the idea of taking our young demons by train all that distance. I doubt if you or I or Rosa would be alive to tell the tale by the end of it. We're going to a hotel first to snatch a meal—once you're through the Customs, that is—then we'll taxi to the airport where I've reserved seats on the next Toronto-bound plane—that's this afternoon. You'll be with Margot and Madge in a few hours—couldn't say just how many, but before bedtime for the kids anyhow.'

"Was I thankful!

"We hustled through the Customs and came on here where we have had the kind of meal you dream about. Oh, my dears! The FOOD! I could wax highly poetical about it if I had the time. But in half an hour the taxis arrive to take us to the airport and I want to finish this instalment first.

"Jack has taken the girls and Steve for a trot round and Michael is having his afternoon nap on the sofa—they call it a 'davenport' here, by the way—with Rosa sitting knitting. Jack offered to take her, too, but she said she'd rather stay. I fancy she feels somewhat overwhelmed with the difference of it all.

"Voices! The crowd are coming back and I'd better pack up and prepare. Mustn't miss that plane. Au revoir! "

Miss Annersley laid aside the sheet and looked round laughingly. "I wish I'd been a fly when Jack met them all. How that wretched girl does torment him! "

"*And* how he torments her!" Matron retorted. "Go on with the letter and reserve your comments for later."

Miss Annersley handed over the remaining sheets to her co-Head. "Hear you are, Nell. My throat's getting rusty."

"Jo certainly seems to have let herself go," Miss Wilson commented as she took the letter. "I *thought* she couldn't have managed all that at one sitting."

"Oh, do go on!" Rosalie pleaded. "I'm expecting a call from Cardiff at any minute now, and I'm having to listen with one ear open for the telephone as it is! "

Miss Wilson nodded and found her place. "Here we are."

56

"Tuesday—*and* Toronto! Well, here we are at last. I have seen everyone and for once I feel satisfied. Margot is a different child. Do you remember the poor little misery that went off with Madge that awful day last April? It was pouring with rain and a half-gale was blowing into the bargain. Margot and the other two had wept copiously from the time they got up and, between losing her *and* Madge, I felt uncommonly like joining the wake party myself.

"There were no tears on this occasion, I promise you! Len and Con have grown enormously, as who knows better than you. But despite Madge's letters, I was somehow expecting to see Margot more or less the same size as she'd left me. You can imagine the shock I got when a Bouncing Bet of a girl came haring up, leapt at me, flung her arms round my neck and had a jolly good stab at strangling me. It shook me more than a little. I can tell you.

"Oh, my dears! Except for her blue eyes and golden mop you wouldn't know her now! She's half an inch taller than either of the others and very much broader. She's completely lost that awful look of fragility that used to worry us so. I don't mind telling you now that there have been times when I've worried myself nearly sick over her. Not even Charles has ever given me so much anxiety. That's all a thing of the past. The doctors here all agree that her health is completely established now and she is as sturdy and robust as heart could wish.

"There was a great meeting between her and the other two. Even my dreamy Con woke up thoroughly—something I was only too thankful to see. Jack is as thrilled as I am. I knew he always watched Margot like a hawk. That need is over—thank God!

"Madge, too, is a different woman. You know, I think she had got into a rut. I'm sure she was in danger of becoming 'That very sweet woman, Lady Russell.' There's a lot more to her than that, as I always knew. She's gone back to Tirol days and is crisp and snappy and brisk, not to speak of looking twenty years younger! A friend of hers came in on Sunday afternoon and you should have seen her face when Madge introduced Sybs as, 'My eldest girl, Sybil—just out from England.'

"The friend regarded Sybs most suspiciously and said, 'You *don't* mean that this is your daughter? I thought she was your younger sister.'

57

"I must say, it looks a lot more like it, now that Sybs has begun to grow up. After all, the kid *is* fifteen now.

"As for the twins, bonny bouncing babies just describes them. Kevin is the image of Jem; and Kester is David over again—including the black Bubbles crop. Madge says they haven't looked back since the word 'Go!' Both are teething but with very little trouble—remember the appalling time I had with Steve? And Mike hasn't been too easy—and they are one long duet of chuckles and crooning when they're awake.

" 'Better train 'em to be crooners for Hollywood when they get a little older,' I suggested.

"Madge raged at me. 'I'll do no such thing! Of all the ghastly ideas! One's for the Army and the other for the Navy—we hope. Anyhow, that's the idea we have for them.'

"I said no more, but went on to congratulating her and Jem on the change in Josette. She's regained all she lost with that awful accident when she was a tiny, and is as sturdy as Margot. As for Ailie, nothing ever ailed her —sorry! That was *not* meant for a pun!—but she's blooming, too. In fact, Canada seems to agree with them all. If only it does the same for Charles, I shall be thankful I agreed to make the break and come.

"Thursday. I'm not going to spend time dilating on Toronto until I've been here a little longer. I'll just say it's a magnificent city and the lake is marvellous. The air really is like champagne—I feel pounds better myself already. I'll just tell you that Madge's house is delightful— perched high above the lake with a garden that is all terraces and steps and stairs. Every terrace is brimming over with flowers and there are the most gorgeous nooks and corners.

"We've sent all the girls to the Convent along with Margot and Josette—the nuns were sweet about taking them—and Steve and Charles go to a kind of K.G. school just round the corner with Ailie; so except for Michael— and Rosa insists on keeping him most of the time—I'm free.

"Jem and Jack insisted on my being overhauled by a doctor pal of Jem's—a very good man, I believe. The result is that I've had to promise I'll go slow and take things easy for the next few weeks. I don't mind admitting that I *have* felt all in lately. What with the entire party going down with severe colds at the beginning of the holidays on top of all the worry of young Con's sleep-walking last term and Grizel's exploits with fire, never to speak of the anxiety about Robin—who is to join us here next month, by the way—I really felt like something that's been to the wash and come back badly ironed! So I'm not sorry to let everything go and have a shot at being a complete lady for a while. All the same, Madge can talk herself black in the face. I *will not* have breakfast in bed every day to please anyone!

"And now, my loves, I'm going to break some news to you in my usual gentle (query) manner. We aren't returning anything like so soon as I told you and honestly expected. The doctors all forbid my attempting the voyage home until the latest addition to the family is well and truly here. That means the middle of October at soonest and if we wait till then, we shall probably stay here for the winter as no one likes the idea of a stormy crossing and the Atlantic can be really nasty by that time, I believe. I don't propose to fly with a new baby to take care of as well as the rest of the family. In any case, Madge has been offered an extension of the lease of their house and is more than half inclined to accept.

"Jem is flying back next month for a few weeks and Jack will take his place later, though he will return in August. One of them ought to be there most of the time. David is to come for the summer holidays, but will return to Winchester when the new term begins. Madge says she has been parted from her eldest son long enough now—she hasn't seen him for more than a year.

"Don't worry about the girls. They can all go on at La Sagesse, so they won't lose any school. As the convent is a French one, they'll probably come back all chattering French like natives. Margot already does that and so does Josette.

"Finally, this will be such a chance to link up with old girls that we haven't seen for years and years. I'm dying to see Corney Flower as a married woman. Evvy Lannis is in New York at present and threatens to descend on us any time now. Finally, Madge has had a long letter from Louise Redmond who is now Louise van Buren and has a jolly little Louette born two months ago. Lulu lives in Vancouver Island where they settled after poor Leonard's death and where she met her husband and she has invited me to go and visit her and meet her latest acquisitions. I'd love the trip and I always was fond of Lulu, so as soon as my own affair is over and the baby is old enough not to mind a spot of flying—aren't we becoming an air-minded family, by the way?—I think I shall go. It may be my one and only chance of seeing the Pacific!

"Anyhow, I think I should be mad not to take all these chances. Think of the books I can get out of them!

"Well, my dears, that's all for the present. I can hear someone say, 'And a blessing, too!' Mind you tell me which of you it was when you write. I'll try to send another screed in a few days' time, when I promise to let myself loose on the scenery. Give my love to everyone.—Jo."

"*P.S.*—I've had to open this because of something I set out to do when I went on with it and on re-reading, find I've forgotten. What's all this yarn about a new girl called Katharine Mary Gordon? I ask because Madge has met an old school friend, a Mrs Gordon now, who is touring in a Musical called 'Puss in the Corner' and has a girl of fourteen or so called Katharine Mary.

"Said Katharine Mary was supposed to be going to school somewhere in Wales—arranged by the lawyers, as Papa is a missionary doctor somewhere out east. One wonders what a missionary was doing to marry a musical comedy actress! Papa is missing and has been for some time, so Mamma has gone back to the stage and was lucky enough to get a chance in this show. The girl was to have returned to England in time for school, but Mamma decided it was a pity for her not to see something more of America, now she's here.

"Madge says Gwen Ferrars, as she calls her, always was a featherbrain, though very charming and dainty. She does whatever comes into her head and is the vaguest creature on this earth when it comes to dates and business letters.

"Madge knows she has Mary-Kate—that's what the kid is called—with her, so who, I ask you, is Katharine Mary?

"I'm assuming of course, that it was the *Chalet* School Mary-Kate was coming to. It certainly looks like it from all you say. Hurry up and answer, for I'm on tenterhooks to find out what it's all about.—J."

Miss Wilson finished and the four people sitting in the

study looked at each other in silence. It was broken by the ringing of the telephone bell and Rosalie Dene leapt to her feet and sped away. Then Matron spoke.

"Well, that's one problem solved, at any rate," she said. "But we *still* don't know if Katharine Mary should have come here in the beginning; or if not, where it is she *ought* to be."

"I don't think we can find that out until we hear from Miss Gordon," Miss Annersley said. "I heard from her bank yesterday and they have no idea where she is. Her last address was Avignon, but a letter sent there has been returned, so now they're as ignorant as we are. I'm very sorry for the Head, who should be responsible for Katharine Mary, but I don't see what else we can do but keep her with us until we have definite information—yes, Rosalie?"

"Mrs Hughes would like to speak to you, Miss Annersley. She has heard about the Swiss scheme and wants to know if you can find room for her elder girl, Gwynneth? You remember that the twelve-year-old, Olwen, is coming here next term."

"Is she holding on? Very well; I'll come." Miss Annersley rose and went to the door. "Distribute all those notes that came with Jo's screed, will you? I'll see you folk at lunch."

The bell rang for Break as she went and the party broke up.

CHAPTER VIII

THE JUNIORS' LATEST

THE problem of Mary Katharine had been solved but that of Katharine Mary was still a puzzle. The authorities, after a long conference among themselves, finally decided to leave the matter as it stood, for the present, at any rate. Short of sending out a broadcast appeal for Miss Gordon to return to her niece at the Chalet School, there seemed to be nothing they could do about making contact with her, and that was much too sensational for the situation.

Wing-Commander Mordaunt, Miss Annersley's cousin, had been duly approached and had, in turn, approached his Foreign Office friend, but without result. Nothing so far was definitely known of the Gordons' fate, though someone had mentioned in a letter home to someone else that Sister Gordon had been imprisoned with a group of Franciscan Missionary Sisters. Of the doctor, there was no trace. News, however, had come that Mary Katharine's father had been imprisoned somewhere in the north.

"What does Katharine herself think?" Miss Wilson demanded.

Miss Annersley looked serious. "She says that she had asked God to look after her people and she means to believe that He will. Poor child! I'm afraid she is going to need every ounce of faith she possesses before this is ended!"

"How long is it since she last saw her parents—or don't you know?" Matron asked.

"Six years, she tells me. That was when Mrs Gordon brought her home to her grandmother. If the worst *should* happen, bad as it may be, it won't hurt so much as if she had been with them recently. Between eight and fourteen there lies a very big gap—mercifully."

Matron nodded vaguely. The Head looked at her curiously. She had paid very little attention to what was being said. In fact, her mind was clearly occupied by something entirely different.

"What are you listening to?" Miss Annersley asked with interest.

"There's something going on upstairs in Wallflower," Matron returned.

"What on earth do you mean?" Miss Wilson asked.

"What I say. Everyone be quiet for a minute and listen."

Dead silence fell. The seven people congregated in the study listened intently. A faint sound of scuffling overhead came to them, and Matron got to her feet.

"Wallflower! I'm going to see what those imps are up to. Go on with your pow-wow; I'll be back in a moment."

She vanished like a flash. Unfortunately, the breeze which was blowing put forth a stronger effort than usual as she left the room and the study door banged behind her. The result was that when she reached Wallflower dormitory, which was over Rosalie Dene's office, she found everyone in bed and asleep—or apparently so. This was what they ought to be seeing that it was after ten o'clock, but Matron looked round suspiciously.

There was a full moon that night, and the silvery light streaming in at the window showed her the two rows of beds, each with its occupant. Some of the heads on the pillows were rather more wildly tousled than seemed quite normal, but apart from that, she saw nothing to which she could take exception.

She withdrew quietly, and waited outside in the corridor for a few minutes. A gentle snore was the only sound that came from the room, so she had to go downstairs unsuccessful. Ten minutes later, if she had only been there to see, bedclothes were tossed back and eight people sat up cautiously.

"Who was it?" someone asked in a breathless whisper.

"Matey. I heard the starch in her dress rustle when she was standing at the foot of my bed," Norah O'Connor, an unregenerate imp from Lower Third, replied.

"My goodness! That was a near thing!" Norah's great chum, Rosemary Smith breathed. "Well, I s'pose we'd better call it a day now. If Matey's suspicious, she's quite likely to come back and we don't want a row."

"I quite thought she'd find out when Lil snored," Norah remarked as she turned round to plump up her pillow. "You are an ass, Lil! You always snore like that when you're excited."

"I don't!" Lilias Hume protested indignantly—and much too loudly to be safe if anyone were within earshot.

The rest hushed her vigorously.

"Shut up, idiot! D'you *want* us to be found out?"

"Someone's coming!" squeaked small Judy Willoughby, one of the youngest in the dormitory.

"Lie down and shut up, everyone!" Rosemary commanded.

With one accord, the eight naughty Juniors flopped back on their pillows and when Peggy Bettany, making the rounds as usual, peeped in to be sure that windows were properly open and all as it should be, it was to find a very correct dormitory.

Peggy withdrew as quietly as she had come, but the ringleaders felt they had better not tempt Providence again that night, especially as both Staff and prefects seemed to be very much on the qui vive tonight. They remained where they were and when Matron, still suspicious of them, peeped in on her way to bed, they were sleeping in good earnest.

Next morning they giggled over their narrow escape while they were dressing. It is certain that if that door had *not* banged when Matron left the study the night before, they would have been well and truly caught, for they had all been far too engrossed in their evil doings to have heard her steps.

"And *then* the fat would have been in the fire!" Norah mentioned airily as she pulled her frock over her head.

With the middle of May, summer seemed to have arrived and the girls all sported the Chalet School uniform of checked brown and white gingham with flame-coloured ties and belts. The frocks, finished off with plain muslin collars and cuffs, were very smart with their straight bodices and widely-flared skirts, but a good many of the Juniors found them trying because Matron would allow only two clean frocks a week at most, so it meant they had to avoid activities guaranteed in their cases to finish off any clean frock in one day.

Norah, granddaughter of a Frenchwoman, pulled her frock into order with deft fingers and then surveyed herself in the long wall-mirror to make sure that she was as trig as possible.

"I can't think how you manage!' Lilias Matthews sighed enviously. "Here's Wednesday and that frock looks almost as clean as when you put it on on Monday. You *are* lucky, Norah! You never seem to get into a mess like me."

Norah retied the bow at the end of her fair plait and turned to look at her chum. "H'm! Yes; that thing does look as if you'd been to bed in it," she commented. "Here; let's see if I can do anything about it."

She knelt down and proceeded to tug at the swinging skirt to straighten it. Then she produced needle and cotton and neatly tacked down the curling points of collar and cuffs. It was an improvement, but Lilias sadly reflected that though it might pass for that day, she must go to Matron for a clean frock at bedtime, and Matron would *not* be pleased.

The Dawbarn twins, a promising pair who were in every piece of mischief the lower school produced, giggled.

"It's a good thing we didn't try last night's stunt in our clothes," Prudence mentioned. "Didn't you bust a sleeve in your 'jama top, Lil?"

The unlucky Lilias nodded mournfully. "I just about did! Matey will be ravers over it. All the same, brightening up as she thought of last night's fun, "it was jolly well worth it. I *nearly* got Rosemary down just before the end. I b'lieve I'd have done it if it hadn't been for Matey barging in."

The young sinners giggled again. Rosemary shut them up.

"If you folk don't hurry, we'll be late and there'll be a row all right for that. Anyway, I'm going to say my prayers now, so shut up, the lot of you."

She plumped down on her knees beside her bed, and the rest, recalled to the day's duties, hurried to finish and follow her example. Even so, they had to rush to strip their beds before they lined up and marched downstairs very properly.

"What were you kids in Wallflower doing last night?" Mary-Lou Trelawney asked when everyone was busy dealing with cereal and milk.

"Doing?" Norah was at her most innocent.

Mary-Lou gave her a grin. "Don't pretend it wasn't you, 'cos I just wouldn't believe it!" she retorted. "I nearly came in to tell you to shut up and let other folk go to sleep."

"Why should you?" Prudence, sitting beyond Norah, demanded. "You aren't a prefect, Mary-Lou—or not *that* sort of prefect." She amended her remark, since Mary-Lou was form prefect for Upper Third, which form she and her twin also graced, though they mainly kept to the bottom while Mary-Lou was always to be found among the top three.

"I always *said* it was a mistake to shove you two Dawbarns into the same dorm," Ruth Barnes observed from Mary-Lou's other side. "Sugar, please, Lala."

Lala Winterton, sitting opposite, pushed the sugar-bowl across and then went on with her chatter with her own special chum, Bess Appleton, who was in the same form. All the same, she had caught a few words which roused her suspicions. Everyone knew that the Dawbarns were as wicked a pair as ever troubled an innocent school; and

Norah O'Connor had plenty of originality and needed no one to egg her on in sin.

Life at the Chalet School was far too full for most people to have a lot of spare time, so it was not until after Mittagessen that Lala remembered what she had overheard at Früstück and looked round for someone to explain to her.

As luck would have it, Mary-Lou came past at that moment lugging her deckchair to her chosen spot for the half-hour's rest stringently insisted on by the authorities.

"Half a sec, Mary-Lou!' Lala called, racing after her.

Mary-Lou stopped short and turned a level blue gaze on the elder girl. "What d'ye want?" she demanded, coming to the point at once as she was wont to do.

"What were you yattering to the Dawbarns and Norah about at brekker—I mean Früstück—about making a noise?" Lala demanded.

Mary-Lou chuckled softly. *"Wouldn't* you like to know? I'm not telling you, Lala. 'Tisn't *your* business. Come to that, I s'pose it isn't mine, either. That all you want? Then I'll get cracking. My crowd are waiting for me."

She departed, leaving Lala to stare after her with a resentment that gradually changed to amusement. Mary-Lou was three years younger than herself, which was partly what had raised the Senior Middle's ire at being spoken to in such an offhand way; but Mary-Lou was constantly doing things like that and getting away with them because, whatever else she intended, she never intended to be impudent.

"Oh, well, I suppose the kid's right and it isn't any of my business," Lala said to herself as she picked up her own chair and went off to join the rest of her form.

All the same, she told her elder sister Polly the whole story when they had a few minutes together later on, and Polly, who was possessed of an outsize in consciences, perhaps because it had wakened late, mentioned the affair to Bride Bettany, head of Upper Fifth and a chum when they were at home.

Bride took it seriously as befitted one who was practically certain of a prefectship next term. "What are those imps up to?" she demanded.

"I wouldn't know, so it's no use asking me," Polly told her. "Something they oughtn't, if Norah and the Dawbarns are in it."

Bride fully agreed with this dictum. It had been Priscilla Dawbarn who, last term, had induced most of the form to sit through prep, moving their jaws as if they were chewing. When Nita Eltringham, the prefect on duty, accused them of chewing-gum offences and commanded them to open their mouths at once for her inspection, the entire crowd, taking their cue from the twins, had promptly and obligingly done so and, furthermore, quite a number had hung out their tongues as far as ever they could. As there was not a shred of chewing gum among the lot, Nita was left to feel that she had made a fool of herself.

Unfortunately for Prudence Dawbarn, they had been so elated with their success with Nita, that several of them had dared to try the same trick on Miss O'Ryan when that lady came to them for history. Biddy O'Ryan had been a demon when she was a Junior at the school and it was very difficult to get away with anything where she was concerned. She had ordered them to swallow anything they might have in their mouths and *then* open them and keep them open while she went the rounds.

Prudence had been foolish enough to take advantage of the mock chewing-gum game to pop a large bullseye into hers shortly before and as she dared not be caught with it and could scarcely disgorge it, seeing she had only just been moved to the front row for bad behaviour, she tried to swallow it. It stuck half-way and she choked so badly, that the alarmed Miss O'Ryan sent for Matron. By the time that bullseye had finally slid down and both Matron and the mistress had finished telling her what they thought of her conduct, Prudence was weeping copiously. Matey, as any of her charges could have told you, had a nasty edge to her tongue on occasion and Miss O'Ryan was past mistress of a form of sarcasm that made you squirm.

"What began it all?" Bride asked.

Polly couldn't say and referred her friend to Lala. All Lala knew was that Mary-Lou and her crowd seemed to be ticking off Norah and the Dawbarns for keeping them awake with their noise.

"Lilias Matthews was in it, too," Lala said.

"So I should imagine. Why on earth Matey ever put that lot together is beyond me!" Bride replied.

"I expect the idea was to have 'em all in one lot so that they didn't spoil two or three dorms," Lala suggested.

"There may be something in that. Well, if anyone in authority catches them out, there'll be trouble. Those Dawbarn twins were born to be hanged and Norah O'Connor isn't far behind them!" Bride said with conviction. "Wasn't that the crowd that were carpeted for pillow-fighting and smashing a window last term?"

"It was," Lala agreed. "They chucked three pillows through an open window, one after the other, just like that—they didn't *break* the window; it was open already—and then they didn't dare to try to go through the house to fetch them. It was pouring with rain when they got down next morning and the pillows were soaked, and Matey was raging."

"Thought I remembered something about it," quoth Bride. She frowned in concentrated thought. "All right, Lal. I'll do something about it myself. No need to drag Peggy and the rest of the prees into it. You keep a still tongue and leave it to me."

"Isn't your kid sister Maeve in with that lot?" Lala asked.

"She is—which is just why I want to leave Peg out of it. She'll feel bound to sit on Maeve harder than the rest, because she's Head Girl and Maeve's her sister, you see. Peg's always terrified of showing any favouritism, so she leans over backwards in the other direction. Maeve's getting to the age when she resents being ticked off by her eldest sister. You leave it to me."

What Bride was feeling after was the fact that Maeve and her twin brother Maurice, who had been born in India, had never seen their elder brothers and sisters until they were eight. Just at first, they had found it difficult to settle in as the youngest members of a big family, Maeve especially. They had settled down finally, but now that Maeve was nearly twelve, the old feeling that Peggy was "coming the eldest sister" over her was returning and there had been two or three unpleasant spats during the holidays.

Peggy was a conscientious girl and tried to help their mother, who was by no means strong, during the holidays. She had taken complete charge of the twins and Maeve had raged at being expected to do as Peggy told her.

Bride knew all this and was anxious not to have anything happen that would deepen this feeling. Therefore, she decided to deal with Wallflower herself.

After consideration, she decided to co-opt two of her friends, so at half-past nine that night, she, Tom Gay, and Julie Lucy crept softly downstrais from their own dormitory, where they should have been preparing for bed, and made for Wallflower.

"What do we do?" Julie murmured as they stood outside for a moment.

Bride opened her mouth to give directions, but before she could say anything, a muffled thud from Wallflower, followed by a triumphant squeak of "I've thrown her— I've done it this time!" focussed their attention.

Bride hesitated no longer. She flung the door open and irrupted into the room, announcing to its horrified occupants, "You're quite right, whoever that was. You certainly *have* done it!"

There was a silence that could be felt after this dramatic statement. The little girls stood where they were, and stared in wide-eyed dismay at their elders. The other two had followed Bride in by this time, and Tom Gay had closed the door softly.

The Juniors had been fearful of Matron catching them, and *that* would have been bad enough. For Bride, Tom, and Julie to break in on them seemed even worse— especially with Bride Bettany, very tall and judicial, standing glaring at them like that. One or two of the weaker vessels burst into tears and sobbed loudly. Rosemary Smith, the Dawbarns, and Norah contrived to overcome any weakness of that kind.

Kicking Gay Spencer who happened to be near her to make her stop, Rosemary turned to the big girls.

"Please, Bride, we weren't doing anything *very* bad," she said in her meekest tones.

"Not doing anything very bad, indeed!" Bride ejaculated. "You were all breaking the Lights Out rule as hard as ever you could go. Do you know what the time is, pray?"

No one did; but in face of Bride's expression, they decided to be silent. Maeve Bettany made herself as small as she could behind Prudence Dawbarn, decided that *all* elder sisters were perfect pests and wished she were back in last term's dormitory.

"What were you doing?" the elder girl asked at length.

"Er—it was ji-you jit-sue," Priscilla replied, pronouncing it more or less as it was spelt.

"Jiu jitsu!" Tom Gay gave a low whistle. "What on earth put kids like you on to such a thing?"

"It was in a book we had for our birthday. There were all sorts of things in it—sports and handcrafts and things like that," Prudence explained. "We thought we'd try it. It might be awfully useful if we ever met with gangsters or burglars or things like that."

Julie Lucy gave Tom Gay an impish smile. "*Much* the best thing to do with burglars—real or imaginary —is to lock them up, isn't it, Tom?"

The little girls were too much upset by their own position to bother their heads about a big girl like Tom Gay, but Bride, giving her a glance, was startled to see that she had reddened to the roots of her boyishly-cropped hair though she said nothing.

"But you mightn't be *able* to get them where you could lock them up," Prudence argued, tempting Fate with a daring that nearly stunned Bride and reduced her own friends to admiration.

Bride, however, swiftly recovered. "That will do. At the moment, kindly realise that you have been breaking rules. I suppose you know what would happen if Matron or any of the Staff or the prefects had happened to catch you?"

As everyone knew, the Juniors kept silence, rightly judging that Bride did not expect a reply.

Tom Gay decided to take a hand. "There's nothing wrong in trying jiu jitsu at the proper time and under proper supervision," she said judicially.

The Juniors gaped at her, wondering what she meant. Bride, sister of three brothers, knew, and promptly pushed the point home.

"My eldest brother told me about a man at his school who broke his arm, fooling round at jiu jitsu," she informed the assembled party. "I believe it's quite easily done."

Silence!

"Then at *that* rate," Julie remarked—*her* brothers were both younger than herself—"I should think they'd better give their word of honour not to play *that* game again."

Tom and Bride agreed.

"You hear, you folk? You can all give us your word

70

of honour that you won't fool round any more with jiu jitsu unless you ask Miss Burn or someone like that to give you a hand. Rosemary Smith, aren't you dorm pree? Promise first, please."

"And hurry up about it," Tom added.

"What'll you do if we don't?" Prudence, who always belied her Christian name, demanded.

The three big girls surveyed her grimly. Bride waited until she was pink and shuffling her feet uneasily. Then she condescended to reply. "Report you to Matey for being out of your beds after Lights Out. Take your choice! Either promise or be reported."

"You *are* a bully, Bride!" Priscilla wailed. "You aren't even a school pree, either," she added resentfully.

"That's nothing to do with it. We're *Seniors*. We're supposed to report anything as flagrant as this and we'll do it unless you swear that you'll stay in your beds after Lights Out in future."

"*And* that you won't go messing about with jiu jitsu in any case," Julie added.

Seeing no help for it, the Wallflower dormitory gave their word sulkily and, after seeing them safely into bed, the Fifth Formers withdrew as quietly as they had come.

Unfortunately for everyone, Matron was on the warpath and, just as the big girls had turned the corner of the corridor and were beginning to mount the stairs to their own dormitory, she shot round another corner, coming full on them.

To meet three girls from Upper Fifth who were supposed to have gone up to bed half an hour ago and to find them fully dressed was something Matron was not prepared to condone. She glared at them and beckoned them to follow to her own room.

"Well, what have you three to say for yourselves?" she demanded. "It's ten o'clock; the bell will ring in another minute; and here you are, on another corridor than your own, and you haven't even attempted to undress. What have you been doing?"

Bride and Co. were in a quandary. They had no intention of giving away the Juniors, yet they had no other excuse that Matron was likely to accept.

"We—we heard a noise and—er—investigated?" Julie finally answered.

"Where?" Matron shot at her.

"Downstairs," Tom replied.

"Well, did you find out what it was?"

"Ye-es," Bride spoke reluctantly.

Matron sat back. "I suppose," she said genially and quite unexpectedly so far as her prey was concerned, "it was Wallflower?"

"Oh, *drat* Matey!" Bride thought indignantly. "Why is she so always on the spot?"

No one said anything, however, so Matron nodded. "I see. Well, I suppose you've settled them, so we'll say no more. All right, girls. In the circumstances, I'll excuse you on one condition—that you tell me, off the record, just *what* those young monkeys were doing."

Bride glanced at the other two. Then she said, "They were trying out jiu jitsu. Those Dawbarns had brought back some book or other explaining it—at least, I think that's the idea. We made them give us their word of honour that they wouldn't do it again unless someone who knew was with them. Rix told us at Christmas about a man in his form who broke an arm trying it. Oh, and they've also promised not to get out of bed after Lights Out."

"Jiu jitsu! Good Heavens!"

"They've promised not to do it again," Tom said. "They're demons, that crowd, but they do keep their word."

Matron nodded abstractedly. Suddenly she looked up. "I shan't take any further notice of it as you three seem to have dealt with them quite adequately. But I shall speak to Miss Annersley about having a private books inspection. Jiu jitsu indeed! I wonder what next!"

That proved to be the Lights Out bell, so Matron sent them off. When they had gone, she rustled off downstairs to report to the highly-amused Staff just what exactly it was that Wallflower had been doing.

Miss Annersley fully agreed that all private literature ought to be inspected and told off Miss Dene, Miss Norman, and Miss O'Ryan to carry it out and impound anything they thought unsuitable.

As among these proved to be the twins' beloved book, they were certainly properly punished and the very name "jiu jitsu" was enough to infuriate the entire octet for the rest of the term.

CHAPTER IX

NEWS AT LAST!

MISS DENE was sorting out the morning mail. It was a lengthy business, since the school numbered well over two hundred pupils and then there were all the teaching and domestic staff as well. First she separated the letters into five heaps—mistresses, domestic staff, Seniors, Middles, Juniors—then she went through the girls' letters again, sorting them out according to the various forms. That done, she banded the piles with stout rubber bands which had to be returned to the office. Finally, she picked out the Heads' and the business letters and then took round everything but those.

She finished with Upper Third, making a mental note as she did so to find out why Mary-Lou Trelawney and her particular crowd seemed to be inundated with sales catalogues and catalogues from all the well-known seedsmen, and was about to deal with Upper Fourth when a letter with an unusual stamp caught her eye. It was addressed to Miss K. M. Gordon and was postmarked Barcelona.

"That's from Miss Gordon!" she exclaimed aloud, stopping short just outside Upper Fourth's door. I must find someone at once!"

She hurried along to the office where she dropped what was left of her bundles into a drawer of her desk, for the window was open and the fresh breeze might easily blow some of them off her desk. Then, with the letter in her hand, she went off to Hall to inspect the time-table.

Miss Wilson was in the science lab, having a coaching with Jean MacGregor, who was taking her first year B.Sc. shortly. From long experience, Rosalie Dene knew that she would object to being disturbed and Jean needed all the coaching she could get, anyhow. The secretary hunted further and discovered that Miss Annersley had the remaining five of Special Sixth for literature in the library.

"Thank goodness for that!" Rosalie thought as she

left Hall and made for the library. "She so easily might have been over at Carnbach."

Miss Annnersley was seated informally on one of the wide window-seats, while her hearers were deployed round her with notebooks and writing-boards, listening eagerly while she helped them to assess the influence of Tennyson on other poets of his time.

Rosalie heaved a small sigh of envy as she entered. There had been no Special Sixth in her day, and in any case, she had left school at just seventeen, owing to the sudden death of her mother. She had kept house for her father, rector of a big city parish, until he married again. Then she had taken her secretarial course and returned joyfully to the school to act as Head's secretary. She was very fond of her step-mother and the small brother who was more than twenty years younger than herself, but she had always felt that she was wise to be away from home for all but the holidays. The second Mrs Dene might have resented a grown-up daughter of the house who was there most of the time.

Rosalie was exceedingly contented with her life; all the same, she wished *she* had had a chance of such lectures as the five who stood up at her entrance were enjoying.

Miss Annersley looked up with a smile. "Want me?" she queried.

"A rather important letter, Miss Annersley," Rosalie replied sedately. "I thought you would wish to attend to it at once."

The Head raised her brows in an eager question and the younger woman nodded. Miss Annerley got up at once.

"Thank you. Will you take it to the study. I'll join you there in a few moments."

Miss Dene withdrew, and the Head, after giving her pupils a few directions, left them to go on by themselves and, once she was out of hearing, ran through the corridors like any schoolgirl, for she guessed what the important letter must be.

"Is it from the Gordons?" she asked as she shut the study door behind her.

"From Miss Gordon, I think. At least, the postmark is Barcelona."

"Almost certainly, then. You were quite right to come

with it at once. Is it for Katharine or the school?"

"For Katharine."

"Let me see." Miss Annersley took the letter and scanned it. "Yes; I'm certain it must be Miss Gordon. Thank heaven! Run and bring Katharine, will you, dear? From all I can gather Miss Gordon is first cousin to a gipsy—here today and gone tomorrow. If this gives us any sort of reliable address, we must get on to her at once."

Rosalie departed and presently returned with Katharine, who was rather anxiously searching her mind for any adequate reason why she should have been called out of algebra to go to the study. So far as she knew she had done nothing wrong.

"Come in, Katharine," Miss Annersley said with a smile. "Here is a letter which must, I think, be from your aunt. You know how anxious we have been to get into touch with her. Open it, my dear, and see if she gives any address to which we can write."

Katharine took the letter calmly enough. She was far too well accustomed to Aunt Luce's gipsyings to be troubled about her going off into the blue for a few weeks and leaving no address. She glanced at the heading. Then she read the first page and suddenly broke into giggles.

"Oh—oh! How exactly like Aunt Luce!"

"Does she give you any address to write to?" the Head asked anxiously.

"Well—she does and she doesn't. She was at Barcelona when she wrote this. She didn't care awfully for Andorra, and came south a fortnight ago. Shall I read it aloud?"

"If you don't mind, dear—No; don't go, Miss Dene. I may need you. Find a chair and sit down. Katharine, there is one for you. Now begin, dear."

Katharine began. " 'Dear Kate,'—That's what Aunt Luce sometimes calls me and always when she writes because it's short," she explained before she resumed. " 'I am in Barcelona at the moment. Andorra wasn't what I'd expected. Scenery grand, but language was a difficulty and I don't think anything of their pubs. I came on here a fortnight ago and have made some quite good studies which I hope to work up later. I have arranged to cross to the Balearic Isles since I am here. I am going with a Spanish fisherman and his sons—fine specimens. I shall make studies of them, too. As I am going on chance, so to speak, I can't give you a definite address, but if you write to me care of the British Consul at Palmas I should get it all right. There is almost sure to be one there.

" 'I have written to the bank to let you draw on my account for any sum up to £20 in case you need money for anything special. You must ask your Head.'—er hum! " Katharine suddenly slurred over the next bit. She could hardly read out what Aunt Luce had written of the Head, which was 'whatever the good woman calls herself; I'm afraid I don't remember," so she hurriedly skipped it and went on, 'to countersign anything you write so that the bank people may know it's all right.

" 'I hope you are enjoying school. I've got a lovely collection of oddments for you from all the places I've visited.' And that's about all," Katharine concluded.

She looked at the Head with blue eyes grown suddenly anxious.

"Well, at least it's an address of some sort," Miss Annersley said briskly. "Miss Dene, you had better send a cable to the British Consulate at Palmas at once. Ask them to contact Miss Lucia Gordon and ask her to get into touch with the Chalet School as soon as possible."

"Yes, Miss Annersley." Rosalie Dene left the room and the Head turned to Katharine.

"What is it, child? Your aunt is quite well, isn't she?"

"Oh, yes. It isn't that. It's—she says nothing about—I suppose she's had no news," Katharine stammered.

The blue-grey eyes that could be so keen, softened magically as the Head said, "I don't think she could possibly. She seems to have been wandering about the Pyrenees district more or less ever since she returned to the Continent. She would hardly be likely to hear anything. In any case, dear, I told you what my cousin had been able to find out, and we *do* know that your mother is safe."

"I know. But—but what about—Father?"

"We are still trying to get word of him. I wish I could tell you that we know more, but I can't. All we can do at present is to hope for the best—and pray that it may be well with him."

Katharine turned to stare unseeingly out of the window, biting her lips to steady them. Unconsciously, she had felt sure that when Aunt Luce *did* write, she would have had news. Now that hope had gone and, plucky girl as she was, it was almost more than she could bear.

Miss Annersley saw that she was fighting for self-control. She knew better than to speak for a moment or two, so the study was very still until the telephone bell suddenly shrilled, breaking the silence.

The Head turned to answer it while Katharine sat struggling with herself. Suddenly, the girl was jerked to attention, for after Miss Annersley had said in her usual quiet voice, "this is the Chalet School. Miss Annersley speaking" her manner changed, her face blazed with excitement, and judging by the staccato conversation that followed, something wonderful had occurred.

"*What*?—Are you *sure*?—*When*?—What are the authorities doing about it?—You're quite certain?—Well, then, I suppose we may expect her very shortly? Can you give me any idea when? No; I suppose not. It's good news, though, and thank you, Edgar, for ringing so promptly. More than I can say!—You haven't any other news, have you?—You have?—Yes—Yes—Well, it's fifth-hand, but at least it's *some*thing!—Thank you.—Yes—How is Gertrude?—Oh, my dear, I'm so very sorry! Give her my love and say I hope she'll be better soon. Poor dear! She does have a time of it! Althea all right—and Nell?—No; I can't possibly manage it for a week or two, anyhow; not until half-term, I'm afraid. I'll come as soon as I can and definitely for that week-end unless something intervenes. Once more, thank you. Good-bye!"

She replaced the receiver on its cradle and came back to Katharine, who had succeeded in pulling herself together.

"Katharine, my dear, I have good news for you."

Katharine looked dumbly at her. She had been quick to guess that Miss Annersley's telephone call must have something to do with her own people, for she knew that Wing-Commander Mordaunt had been trying to find out something about them. She was still shaken by the shock of realising that Aunt Luce, at any rate, had no news, so she felt herself unable, in the reaction that was affecting her, to say a word.

Miss Annersley knew this. She sat down beside the girl.

"That was my cousin, dear, and he tells me that the Franciscan nuns with whom your mother was, are to be sent to Hong-Kong, and the other women who were with them. That means that your mother will be free shortly if

77

she isn't already. They are to be flown home as soon as possible, though my cousin can't say just when; but soon. Best of all, there is news of your father."

"News of Dadda?" In her overwrought condition, Katharine reverted to the old baby name.

The Head watched her expressive little face closely as she said, "Yes, my child. It is at fifth-hand, but at least it is better than the long silence. My cousin has been told that the report is that your father was flown to Chinchow in Manchuria, and is working there at his old job."

"Do you mean that he's free, too?"

"No; I don't think it means that, exactly. But it does mean that he will have fair treatment—far better than he would have received in a prison. My cousin's informant said that the report was that Dr Gordon was fit and well."

Katharine stared at her dazedly. Despite her own statement that she trusted in God and knew He would keep her parents safe, she had been living under a much heavier strain than she had realised. This sudden relief was more than she could take calmly. The tears came in a storm of sobs and the Head held her close without saying anything.

It was a regular tempest, and Katharine cried till she was exhausted, but when at last she sat quiet with her head on Miss Annersley's shoulder, she felt better than she had done for the past few weeks.

"That's better," the Head said at last as she put her own clean handkerchief into Katharine's hand. "Dry your eyes, dear, while I ring for Matron. I think the rest of the day on a bed will be the best thing for you, and you shall go to San. where you will be quiet."

She rang the bell for Matron and when that lady arrived, quickly explained matters to her. "We have had news of Katharine's parents at last, Matron. It's good news, but the relief from the strain has upset her, so I want you to tuck her up on the window bed in San. for the rest of the day. A glass of hot milk, I think, and then I hope a good sleep to follow and she will probably feel much better; but just now her head is aching with crying and she feels tired."

"H-how did you know?" Katharine asked with a hiccough.

Miss Annersley laughed. "My dear girl, I've been Head of this school for a good many years now—and I was a

78

schoolgirl myself in the dark ages. I haven't forgotten. Now go with Matron and try to get that sleep I spoke of and you will feel as right as rain by tea-time."

She drew Katharine to her and kissed the tear-wet face. The girl clung to her for a moment. "Oh, I'm so glad and so—so *muzzy*. But I *said* I knew God would look after them and He did—He *did*!"

"He always does if we could only learn to trust Him. Now go with Matron, darling, and don't worry any more. Just rest and thank God."

Matron took Katharine off, tucked her up on the bed standing close to one of the sunny windows in the school San. and, after standing over her till she had drunk a big glass of hot milk, left her with a pat and an injunction to go to sleep.

"Don't try to get up till I see you again. A day's holiday from lessons won't hurt you for once. Bless you, child!"

She left the room, certain that the worn-out girl would be sleeping soundly before long. Half an hour later, she looked in to find that Katharine was fast asleep and already looked more like herself, despite her swollen and reddened eyes.

In the meantime, cables had gone flying to Palmas to give Miss Gordon the good news and the two Heads realised thankfully that the problem of Katharine Gordon was well on the way to being completely solved.

CHAPTER X

CAMP—AND JELLYFISH!

"ARE you ready, girls? Atten-TION!"

The First Chalet School Company of Guides came smartly to attention and Miss Burn, who was their Captain, surveyed them with a twinkle.

"Talk of puppies straining at the leash!" she murmured in an aside to her two lieutenants, Miss O'Ryan and Miss Bell. "*Look* at 'em!"

Aloud, she said, "You march quietly through the

kitchen-garden, orchard, wheatfield, and lane. When you reach the rough on the cliffs, you still march until you are at the head of the cleft. There you wait until you're told what to do next. Company—TURN!"

The Company turned as one girl, watched by the envious eyes of the Second Company, and such unfortunates who, for one reason or another, were neither Guides nor Rangers, and the Brownies. Miss Wilson, who was District Commissioner for Carnbach Guides and who had a Commissioners' meeting at the County Headquarters, thus unable to accompany the First, stood at the wide door watching them, very trig in her uniform.

"Forward—MARCH!"

The Guides marched off with a steady tramp round the house, through the kitchen garden and orchard, down one side of the wheatfield, green with the vivid emerald of the young wheat, and out into a little lane. Along this they went, headed by the handcart which was in the charge of the Oaks, across a narrow valley through which meandered a brook, and up the steep slope of rough pasturage until they reached the gorse-strewn land at the clifftop. They crossed this to the head of a narrow rocky cleft down which led the path that took them to Kittiwake Cove, their own private bathing-place. Here they were halted by Miss Burn, who had only waited for a last word with Miss Wilson and then come round by the road on her bicycle.

"Handcart first," the Captain said. "Tom, can you get it down, do you think?"

Tom Gay, Patrol Leader of the Oaks, took a comprehensive survey of the steep, rugged path and then nodded.

"Yes, Captain. It'll take a bit of manhandling, but I reckon we can do it safely enough. I'll have the Colours off, though," she added. "And the tent-poles. Don't want to smash them up by jabbing them into a rock."

"Very well," Miss Burn agreed. "Beeches—or no; Laburnums, please."

The Laburnums, headed by Julie Lucy and Elfie Woodward, marched forward to take charge of the flagstaffs and tent-poles, and then the Oaks began on their decidedly tricky job.

When they were half-way down, the Captain gave the Laburnums the word and they followed with their almost as awkward burdens, for the path turned and twisted and at no place did it lie open, the rocky walls rising on either hand and well above the heads of the younger girls.

The Poplars, who were to take charge of the cooking, went next, led by Bride Bettany, who was an old hand at camping, and Elfie Woodward, a great friend of hers. They had the baskets containing the crockery; and the Cherries and Beeches who came last bore the food, since the handcart was loaded to capacity with the tents, palliasses, and blankets.

Besides the First Company, half the Cadet Company were there, too, but they had gone half an hour before and when the Guides reached the warm golden sand they found a big driftwood fire already blazing away with Peggy Bettany and Daphne Russell tending it, while further along at the foot of the cliffs, the remaining six wrestled with the second cadet tent.

"Good!" Miss Burn said as she surveyed the results of the cadets' labours. "Poplars, if you really want to make stew you'll have to set to work. Cherries, bring your baskets here and put them down on that flat rock. Then be off with you to gather driftwood. Bring dry stuff first, please. This fire needs feeding."

"May we take our sandals off, please?" Primrose asked.

"By all means. Don't try any venturesome tricks. There is plenty of stuff lying about over there at the foot of the cliff and it ought to be bone dry by this time."

The Cherries, of which patrol Katharine and Hilary were both members, squatted down to toss off their sandals and then went racing off to begin their work.

Having made arrangements for feeding them all, Miss Burn turned her attention to the tents. Dickie Christy was going round with a huge mallet, knocking in tent-pegs as firmly as she could. The Captain summoned the rest of the cadets, set them in charge of the three remaining patrols and bade them see to setting up the big commissariat and recreation tents first and the sleeping tents after. She and her lieutenants turned their attention to the bell-tent they would share.

It was a busy scene and the girls all worked hard—a good deal harder than some of them quite realised.

"It seems an awful lot to have to do for just two days and one night," lazy Hester Layng observed as she helped to wrestle with the canvas.

"Rot!" said Peggy trenchantly. "If we're going to camp

we ought to do it properly, no matter how long the camp lasts. You *are* a slacker, Hester."

"I like a quiet life," Hester informed her calmly.

"No need to tell us that," Dickie told her as she arrived with the mallet, having undertaken to see that all tent-pegs were properly driven in. "Haven't you people got any further than this? What a set of slugs you are!"

"You try to get a move on with a pack of Junior Middles yapping round from every point of the compass *and* someone like Hester, who prefers a quiet life," Peggy replied tartly. "*No*, Ruth! Leave those guy-ropes alone. We aren't ready to tighten them yet. Think the centre-pole is safe, Dickie? It seems a trifle wobbly to me."

"Run and bring the handcart along, Priscilla," Dickie ordered after she had tested the pole. "I'll give it a good bang or two with the mallet and that'll steady it?"

"The handcart?" Nancy Chester, leader of the Beeches, asked with eyes dancing.

Big Dickie was, perhaps, the most good-tempered girl that ever entered the Chalet School: "No, idiot!" she retorted with a chuckle. "The pole! I suppose you don't want it to descend on you half-way through the night?"

"I do not! I've had that experience once and it was more than enough!" Nancy went off and presently came pushing the handcart through the soft sand with visible effort.

Dickie pulled it into position, mounted it, and proceeded to bang the top of the pole with hearty goodwill.

"That better?" she called.

"Much better, thanks. Stretch the tent, Guides, and wait till I come before you start messing with the guy-ropes."

By the end of an hour and a half, the tents were all up. An incinerator to burn the rubbish had been started in a deep hole and dinner was ready. Miss Burn, who had been here, there, and everywhere, supervising everyone's effort, blew the "Freeze" on her whistle and when everyone except two or three of the Cherries who were at the far end of the cove gathering fuel had arrived, she issued her orders.

"Wash at the spring; then bring your plates and mugs and line up in patrols. Hurry!"

They hurried. The savoury smell coming from the big dixies on the camp hearth had suddenly made them realise that they were famished and no one, not even Hester, loitered.

They lined up, armed with plates and mugs and were served with ladlefuls of stew by Bride, potatoes by Elfie, and lemonade by Mary-Lou Trelawney and Verity-Ann Carey. Then they went to seek places round the long strips of white American cloth which served as tablecloths and for a short time most folk were too busy to talk much.

The second course was ripe gooseberries from the kitchen-garden and when the last gooseberry had vanished and Grace been said, the Laburnums cleared away and washed up while the Poplars retired for a much-needed rest.

Cherries went off for more driftwood, for they must have a good stack or else give up their afternoon later on to replenishing the heap. The rest either helped with this or cleared up any oddments left lying about.

"What comes next?" Katharine demanded as she and Hilary plodded back over the hot sand with their arms full of driftwood.

"Rest," Hilary said briefly. "Thought you'd been a Guide for ages?"

"So I have, but we never camped somehow. What after rest?"

"Goodness! *I* don't know. You'll have to ask Burnie. Bathe, with any luck, I should think." Hilary tossed down her last armful on the great heap they had collected, an example followed by Katharine, and proceeded to mop her hot face. "Phew! It's cooking hot!"

"Make up the fire to last a bit, Cherries," Miss Burn came over to them. "Go and sponge your hands and faces and after that lie down somewhere in the shade. Rest for the next half-hour or so."

Assisted by the rest of the patrol under the watchful eye of Primose, they built up the fire scientifically. Then their leader carefully smothered it with some turfs brought for the purpose and stood up, dusting off her hands.

"That's all for the moment—thank goodness! That'll burn a goodish while and when we want it we've only to take the turfs off and rake the ash away, and we'll have a beautiful clear fire in no time. Go and sponge, you folk. The whistle for rest will go in a moment."

They hurried off to the spring which bubbled out of the

rock half-way up the cliff and ran down in a silver trickle till it was lost in the sand.

"Wish we could have a good sluice," Carola Johnston, the patrol Second, grumbled. "Every blessed thing I have on is sticking to me!"

"I expect we'll bathe after rest," Primrose said soothingly. "Anyhow, Burnie told you just to sponge, so don't you start any tricks, young Carola."

Carola grunted, wiped her hands and face and then departed to seek her chum Jean Ackroyd, who had been helping with the washing-up. Katharine and Hilary hunted out a shady spot under a rock pinnacle and sprawled full length on their backs. Hard work, the hot day and a good, substantial meal all combined to make them drowsy and before long half the company were fast asleep and the others lay drowsing.

Katharine clasped her hands behind her head and gazed up at the blue sky flecked lightly with fleecy clouds. Hilary at her side was frankly and unashamedly asleep and none of the rest of her crowd were near. The girl gave herself up to wondering when her mother was likely to arrive in England and when the news about her father would be fully confirmed.

It was a week since the first tidings had come and she had completely recovered now. Aunt Luce had been heard from that morning and had announced that she was returning as soon as she could, so all was very well with Katharine's world at the moment. With a deep sigh of satisfaction she rolled over on her side and fell into a half-doze.

Half an hour later, the whistle went and the silence came to a speedy end. The sleepiest person was wide awake in less than a minute and when Miss Burn announced that bathing was the next item on the programme, they set up a cheer that was heard at school.

"How many of you have passed the test? Hands up!" the Captain ordered.

A forest of hands waved madly. Since the school had come to the island everyone was taught swimming, and most of them had passed the test, though there were one or two new girls and some who had not had many lessons who still could not swim the distance Miss Burn had insisted on.

"Very well," she said. "All who can may change and

84

go in at once. Mind you remember my rules or you don't go in again this camp. Hilda—Gillian—you two Dawbarns —Lala Winterton—and—oh, yes; Dilys Enderby and Dorothea Fletcher you may change and wait until I come to you. Off you all go!"

They scattered and, five minutes later, the shore was thronged with girls in the Chalet School white bathing-suit and helmet, though a good many of those lucky enough to have short hair dispensed with the last.

The rules were few but stringent. No girl might go further than a certain rock about a hundred yards out and no girl might go that far alone. They might not enter the water until the boats, manned by either prefects or Staff, had taken up their stations at various strategic points. No girl was allowed to go in without a mistress until she had passed the test. At the first blast of the recalling whistle you had to make for shore at once or forfeit your bathe next time.

Miss Burn, having seen the school's boats manned and pulling in leisurely fashion to their stations, ran to change, and when she appeared quite two-thirds of the girls were already splashing in the water and most of the others were racing to join them. Her own six were squatted on the wet sand waiting for her.

"I'll take you first, Lala," she said briskly. "Come along and let's see if you can pass the test today. If you can, you can join the others at once."

She led the way and presently Lala was waistdeep in the water beside a flat-topped rock on which the Captain stood while she instructed her pupil. "Off! Take your time and don't splash so—Prudence and Priscilla, stop fooling or you'll go out at once!—oh, good, Lala! Half-way point! Keep going and I believe you'll do it today!"

Lala, who was keen enough, but who had never, so far, managed to swim the required distance, forged bravely ahead and was rewarded by hearing the mistress shout, "Well done! You've passed! Now you can go and join the others. Don't go further out, though, until you can do it quite easily."

With a glow of satisfaction, Lala stood up in the water and Miss Burn went off to take the Dawbarns, who had had only three lessons so far but were shaping well. They kicked out with small regard for style but much goodwill and managed to swim twenty strokes unaided, after which she sent them inshore with strict orders not to come further than hip-deep and turned to Hilda Jukes.

In the meantime Katharine, having learned to swim at almost the same time as she learned to walk, struck out with a strong trudgeon that sent her through the water like an arrow, leaving Hilary far behind.

Peggy Bettany, disporting herself at the hundred-yard limit with her own friends, watched her coming, treading water vigorously.

"That kid can swim," she said to Daphne Russell. Then she raised her voice. "Hi, Katharine! Come and have a race! Dick-ee! —Ni-ta!"

Dickie and Nita, who were practising surface diving near by, came swimming up and Peggy looked round for a starter.

Daphne saw Hester, who always described herself as "a contemplative swimmer," by which she meant that racing was not in her line, though she could swim well enough when she chose.

"Hester!" The editress of the school magazine raised her voice in a shout. "Come and be starter for us!"

Hester heard and, turning over, swam up to them. "What's cooking?"

"A race between us five. Will you start us?" Peggy asked, coming to the point with characteristic brevity.

"So long as you don't ask me to join in," Hester agreed. "Better start from the Table, hadn't you? I can stand there and the water's deep enough for a dive. Half a sec!" She scrambled out of the water on to the rock to which the others also swam, "Up you get! Energetic beings! It's a pity Joan is in the other Company, isn't it? However!"

They made a line along the top of the rock, Hester standing at the far end, and waited with arms ready.

"Better mind you don't topple off," Peggy advised the starter. "You're standing awfully near the edge."

Hester made a face at her. "Are you read-ee? Get read-ee," she intoned. "GO!"

She flung up one arm on the last word and the five promptly dived. Hester made a careless step and also went in, to come up choking and gasping for she had swallowed an unpleasant amount of salt water. The racers paid no attention to her, however. In fact, they had not seen the accident, for at the moment that she went over backwards, they had all touched water and were all striving to surface as far as possible from the Table. Hester strugged back, puffing and blowing and then stood up to watch the race.

All five swam well, but Nita Eltringham and Katharine Gordon were clearly best. They quickly outdistanced the others and it was a neck and neck fight between them.

Hester had had no need to ask the course of the race, for such impromptu events always took the same way— right round a big, jagged tooth known as the Minstrels' Rock because, so legends said, a certain heathen chieftain of King Arthur's day had bound together the Christian minstrels of a rival, tied them to the rock and left them to drown in the rising tide. The doomed men had sung hymns until the water silenced them, and the chieftain himself, watching their slow death from a small boat, had been caught in the trough of a great wave that rose out the sea unexpectedly, and hurled to his own end against the cruel peak of the rock.

Katharine and Nita rounded the rock almost side by side and then settled down for the homeward struggle. A minute later, Peggy came round it, followed at a short distance by Daphne and Dickie.

The girls near at hand had stopped their own fun to watch; and it is on record that Mary-Lou was so excited that she forgot she was out of her depth, simply stopped swimming and went under with a strangled yelp. Luckily, she was a veritable little fish and Clem Barrass was near enough to grab at her and yank her head clear again, so no harm was done.

Miss Burn removed her eyes from the non-swimmer for a moment and Hester, forgetting her laziness for once, danced a wild fandango on the Table Rock in her excitement.

And *that* was the moment that Priscilla Dawbarn chose to stumble into a group of half a dozen jellyfish that were floating in on the tide. She grabbed at one, was instantly and agonisingly stung and uttered a shriek that outdid anything so far produced. To make matters worse, she tried to back in a hurry, tripped and went under, coming up in the very middle of the group.

Priscilla's screams sent Miss Burn flying to the rescue and only the common sense of Bride Bettany and Nancy Chester, who grabbed her firmly between them, kept

Prudence from doing the same thing and complicating matters.

Miss Burn plunged in, caught Priscilla and dragged her out of her very unpleasant situation, but not before the child had been badly stung and she herself had also suffered.

"Best take her straight back to Matron," Miss O'Ryan said. "Jellyfish stings are no joke. Can you manage or shall I take her?"

"I'll take her—and two of the Seniors can come with us," Miss Burn gasped.

The history mistress glanced round. "Tom Gay—and Bride Bettany!" she said. "Get your wraps and sandals on and help Miss Burn and Priscilla back to school."

The pair set off at once and presently the quartette were struggling up the cleft, the stalwart Seniors carrying a sobbing, writhing Priscilla between them while Miss Burn scrambled up by herself, feeling rather sick as the poison from her stings sent the pain through arms and legs.

Miss O'Ryan, left alone since Miss Bell, the other Lieutenant, had taken over the frantic Prudence and had her hands full with her, blew the "Return!" on her whistle and the girls came crowding in, giving the jellyfish a wide berth.

The history mistress issued commands that the girls were to keep out of the water for the present and suggested that they should see about tea so that it would be ready when Miss Burn returned.

"The worst of it is," Peggy said disgustedly later on, "we never finished the race, for naturally, when we heard Priscilla's howls, we all turned and made for shore, so we still don't know whether Nita or Katharine is best."

"Never mind," the Captain said soothingly—it was after tea and she had rejoined them, still rather pale, but otherwise her usual self. "As the Spaniards say, 'Tomorrow is also a day.' You can have your race tomorrow evening, by which time I hope the tide has carried those creatures elsewhere."

"And I don't mind telling you," Miss O'Ryan added thoughtfully, "that I'm sorry she had such a nasty experience, but it's myself is a thankful woman to be relieved of *one* Dawbarn anyhow. Why ever were those two allowed to join the same Company? I call it tempting Providence, myself."

CHAPTER XI

ONE OF THE TENNIS SIX

JOAN SANDYS, the Games prefect, was sitting at the big table in the prefects' room, scribbling hard with intervals for chewing the end of her pencil. Peggy, Daphne, Nita, and Dickie were perched on the table at the window, chattering like magpies about the half-term weekend which was due the weekend after next. Most of the girls were going home; and those who lived too far away were either going off with friends or were to be taken by some of the Staff for a motor-coach tour of North Wales. Dickie, whose home was in St Briavel's, was one of the latter, and Daphne and Nita were going to North Devon with Peggy.

Suddenly, Joan looked up. "I do wish you folk would stop yattering!" she burst out. "I simply can't *think* with all the noise you make!"

Startled, the four turned with one accord to see what she was doing.

"*Not* prep, I hope, after all Miss Annersley said," Peggy observed in shocked tones.

"Don't be a bigger idiot than you can help!" Joan retorted. "No; I'm trying to fix up the Tennis Six. We play Campden House on Saturday as you may or may not remember, and you know what that young ass Mollie has done to her wrist. And just as if that wasn't enough, Matey sent for me after tea to tell me that Julie Lucy was down with tummy-pains and unlikely to be fit for anything much before Monday! Elfie is our first reserve and she's going home on Friday to see some relative or other who is on his way from Canada to Cape Town and wants to see her. Hasn't set eyes on her since she was a howling infant and is curious to know how she's grown up, if you please. Anyhow, she's out of it and I simply don't know *what* to do about the Six."

"Is it a Home or Away match?" Nita asked. "And what's this about Julie?"

"Matey said tummy-pains," Joan replied briefly.

Nita looked disturbed. "I don't like that. The kid's been having pain off and on ever since we came back, only the little ninny wouldn't go to Matey though I told her to. I hope there's nothing really wrong."

"Matey murmured something about a grumbling appendix—whatever that may mean," Joan said. "As for the match, it's Home, so we certainly want to put up a decent showing. They beat us both times last season, you may remember."

"Who've we got definitely?" Nita demanded, abandoning Julie and her appendix for the moment.

"Well, Peggy—Daph—you. Then we have either Nancy Chester or Gisel Mensch, but we can't have both. One of them must captain the Second Eleven against Carnbach Grammar. I'm going with the First to the Sacred Heart at Terrington, and anyhow, tennis isn't really my game. It truly is the most ghastly mess-up!"

"What about Anthea Barnett? She's jolly good on her day," Dickie suggested. She herself was also playing for the First Eleven and, in any case, like Joan, tennis was not her game.

"She hasn't been on her form for the past fortnight. I don't know what's wrong with her, but I simply daren't risk it. She might come off—or she might not. Campden House wiped up the earth with us that second match last season so I do want to give them our very best. If they beat us again this year, they'll think we're complete duds and neither challenge us nor accept our challenges again."

"Who's being the idiot now?" Peggy demanded. "We don't stand or fall by what happens in one or two matches but by our average on the season. Besides, didn't Campden House have that pair of sisters who got into the Junior Championship semi-finals last summer?"

"They did; and they've both left," Daphne said. "One was going to Cambridge in October, and the other was going in for nursing. Whatever happens, we shan't have *them* to face, thank goodness!"

"There you are!" Peggy chimed in again. "This mess-up of the teams seems to have affected your brain, Joan, my love. Snap out of it! We've plenty of other averagely decent players. What about—well, what about that Upper Fourth tennis demon, for instance?"

"Katharine Gordon? I did think of her, but she's awfully

young, Peggy, not quite fifteen. Do you think she has the stamina for matches? I know she's good—in fact, out-standing—but do you think she could carry three match sets straight off?"

"Oh, come off it, Joan!" This was Dickie's contribution. "The kid's bigger than Peggy and has a service like a man's. I should say she has all the stamina she's likely to need. But if you want to make sure," she added, "why on earth don't you try her out? Let's see: what day is it?"

"Wednesday!" three voices said together.

"There you are, then. Go into a huddle with Burnie about it and see if she can't get excuses from prep for some of us and young Katharine and test her out after tea."

"And," added Nita, "put Natalie Mensch in. That music school of hers is over now so she'll be free to put in a good spot of practice and she did play for the Six last season."

"That's an idea. I'd forgotten about Natalie." Joan scribbled down the name and then thought. "That would give us you and Peggy for first couple; Daph and Natalie for second, and either Nancy or Gisel with Katharine Gordon—if she's good enough—for third.

"I'd put Nancy in," Dickie advised. "I don't think the Second will want to lose Gisel's bowling. She's come on a lot lately and those twisters of hers ought to go a long way towards helping to win that match."

"The rest of you agree to that?" Joan looked round and received a series of nods. "O.K., then. Katharine and Nancy for third pair. And look here; what do you think about putting in Blossom Willoughby as a reserve? She's quite good, you know."

Peggy considered. "I think I'd test the pair of them against each other and put whichever wins into the pair and let the other play reserve. Who for second reserve? We'd better make sure of that. We seem to have struck a bad patch, what with young Elfie's loving relatives and Julie's tummy-pains."

"Primrose—no; she's Second Eleven. Well, what about Anthea?" Daphne proposed.

"Mightn't she feel rather—well, rather insulted?"

"Not she! Anthea's got sense. You go and see what she says."

"O.K., I will," Joan agreed. She stood up and stretched

herself. "Thanks a lot, all of you. I'll go and find Burnie and see what she says when she sees the list."

"I hope you mean to fair-copy it first," Dickie remarked with a grin. "If you hand her that scrawl, she'll probably suggest that you'd be the better for a few copies!"

Joan glanced at her scribbled list and laughed. "Perhaps I'd better. Burnie's a dear, but she can flay you alive with her tongue when she chooses!"

She sat down with a fresh sheet of paper and copied her list. Then she jumped up and ran off in search of Miss Burn, who was down at the tennis courts superintending a set between Blossom Willoughby and Gwen Parry against Katharine Gordon and Madge Watson, Joan paused to watch the players and was duly impressed by the performances of all four.

"Gwen and Madge have come on a lot," she thought. "Blossom is much steadier this year, too. As for that Gordon kid, it wouldn't surprise me if she reached Wightman Cup standard before she's finished. For her age, she's excellent."

The four in question never noticed the Games prefect. They were far too intent on their game. Miss Burn was trying them out with an eye to inter-house matches. These took place the last full week of term and all four knew they stood a very fair chance of being chosen for Ste Thérèse's, as that house had few really good players among the elder girls, who seemed to be mainly cricketers this season.

The game ended in a victory for Blossom and Gwen when deuce had been called four times and Madge ended it by tamely sending her return into the net. While they changed ends for the second half of the practice, Miss Burn saw Joan and came over to her.

"Anything wrong?" she asked. "Or have you just come down to take notes?"

Joan explained the dilemma in which she had found herself and the solution she and the others proposed, and the Games mistress agreed at once.

"It's a nuisance all three matches falling on the same date. However, that's a good idea. I'll go and see about leave for Blossom and Katharine for this evening later on. Will you take the Lower Third for me? Then I can go when this hour's ended."

"I'd like to. It's a free afternoon for me and I ought

to have some idea of how those babes are progressing. Shall I get one or two of the others to come down as well? Then we could keep three courts going and have one person to watch at the practice-boards."

"Excellent! I must go now, Joan. These people are ready for me." Miss Burn turned back to her duty and Joan ran off to collect helpers for Lower Third tennis.

The result of Miss Burn's appeal was that Katharine and Blossom were excused from preparation that evening and came down to the practice-courts agreeably excited. They found Joan there with Peggy and two or three more of the Sixth, waiting for them.

"Miss Burn says we'd best try you out on the match courts," Joan said. "She's waiting there for us. One of us will partner each of you in a full doubles set. Then you'll play off five singles games. Come on!"

Arrived at the important match courts, the Sixth Formers tossed up to see who should play with the younger girls. Nita and Anthea won, so partnered the rather nervous pair while the others sat round and watched with eagle eyes for faults.

This made it rather nerve-racking for the younger girls, and Blossom, who served first, began by foot-faulting badly. Katharine made no mistakes, but she played very cautiously and showed none of her usual brilliance. The game was won by Nita and Blossom, thanks mainly to Nita's drives. Then the pair crossed over and Katharine was facing service.

Blossom's first ball was out of court and her second a tame lob which Katharine treated as it deserved, driving it into the farthest corner of the opposite court where Nita tried to reach it but just failed, so that the first point went to Anthea and Katharine. They won that game and the next. Then Blossom suddenly seemed to recover and the entire set was a regular battle for points. It went eventually to Anthea and Katharine, the latter's cunning placing and nasty drop-shot returns proving a little too much for her opponents while Anthea played a sound if rather uninspired game in support.

"Five minutes' rest," Miss Burn said when she had announced the result. "Then I'll see Katharine and Blossom in a singles. Katharine, is that racquet of yours all right? It looks to me as if one of your strings wasn't too safe."

"Have mine?" The Sixth spoke in a chorus as they held out their racquets.

Katharine examined her own, realised that the mistress was right and, after "hefting" one or two of the others, chose Peggy's which was the same weight as her own.

Perhaps it was because she was using a strange racquet that her play during the first two games of the singles was a very tame affair. She made no mistakes, but Blossom found it an easy matter to return her balls, winning a love game first, though the second went to thirty-forty before a nasty drop-shot gave it also to her.

"And that," said Peggy to Joan, isn't good enough. She's a long way better than Blossom really, even though that monkey seems to have the makings of a decent player in her. Let's hope young Katharine recovers her form this next game."

By that time, however, Katharine was becoming more used to the feel of the racquet, and though Blossom took the game to deuce no fewer than five times, it went to the new girl in the end.

The last two games were a very different affair from the first two. Katharine had regained her proper form and she had Blossom racing all over the court. They had some fierce rallies and Miss Burn privately noted that Blossom's volleying had improved out of all recognition this season. All the same, Katharine had that little bit extra that tells and she won both games handsomely. That settled the matter. Blossom came in as one of the reserves and Katharine was to partner Nancy Chester in the third pair for Saturday's match.

CHAPTER XII

TROUBLE IN UPPER FOURTH

THE Chalet School had a good many interests apart from lessons and games. Among these, and very important, was gardening. Such girls as wished to make a career of it spent their last year at school in training for Swanley and kindred establishments under Miss

Everett, the gardening mistress. "Evvy," as the school at large called her—though never to her face!—was an experienced gardener and the girls under her did well when they went on to more intensive training.

In addition, since labour was always a difficulty, it had been decided when the school first moved to the island that the seven upper forms must be responsible for the flower gardens and part of the kitchen garden. Special Sixth were in charge of the rose garden; the Sixth prided themselves on their salads of all kinds; the three Fifths had undertaken the front garden with its great lawns, studded with clumps of flowering shrubs and its beds and borders of herbaceous flowers. The two Fourths were responsible for the rock garden on the south side of the house and the herb patch respectively. The rest of the school were allowed to have form beds where they might do as they pleased on the north side of the house; but during term-time, at any rate, the elder girls were expected to accept full responsibility for their form allocations.

Upper Fourth as a whole were very proud of their flowers and on most possible evenings there were generally half a dozen or so of them at work in the rock garden where they did not confine themselves to rock plants only, but insisted on making pockets of deep earth wherever they could and growing herbaceous flowers as well.

On the day after Katharine and Blossom had achieved the honour of being chosen to represent the school at tennis, they, together with Hilary, Meg, Elinor, Madge, and Hilda, were all hard at work there.

The two tennisites, as Hilary had promptly dubbed them, had been out at seven that morning, having a practice set and had also had a good practice that afternoon, so Miss Burn had refused to let them play again in the evening.

"You don't want to overtire yourselves," she had told them. "You run along and play somewhere—but *not* tennis!"

Wherefore Katharine and Blossom might have been found cleaning up the pansy-border which it had pleased the form to plant right along both sides of the central path. Madge and Hilda were weeding along the top of the rockery; the other three were engaged in staking lupins, delphiniums, hollyhocks, and such other tall plants as they had coaxed to grow in their earth pockets which were mainly in the corners so as not to overshadow the smaller rockery plants.

It must be owned that Katharine was no asset to the form where gardening was concerned. Most of her life had been spent in a London flat, and after she had industriously pulled up a whole row of seedling Sweet Williams under the impression that they were weeds, she had, with one accord, been ordered to keep to such obvious things as needed no one to keep perpetual watch on what she was doing.

"*Why* do we have to pull off all the dead pansies?" she suddenly asked Blossom.

"Search me! Because Evvy says we've got to, I suppose," replied Blossom, who was not keen, but did her share as a natural result of being a member of the form.

"It's because if you don't, the wretched things start seeding and that means no more flowers—not on those plants, at any rate," Hilary explained from a little further away where she was engaged in staking a young hollyhock.

"But you don't do it to things like—well, like irises," Katharine objected, her eye being caught by a mass of blue irises of every shade that grew in a sunk tub to one side of the path.

"Oh, they come from bulbs or crowns or something like that and spread that way," Hilary said vaguely as she tied her last knot. "There! That should be safe enough now!"

"Then you'd better see about staking the big delphinium," said Miss Everett's voice behind her. "I've put Elinor on to sticking those sweet-peas you insisted on having at the far corner. I must say you people seem to like work! I suppose you realise that if we have any dry weather you'll have to water those sweet-peas every day? Well, it's your own concern."

"We gave them lots of earth, though, Miss Everett," Hilary said.

"That won't save you from having to water. Mind you clear all those dead pansies, Katharine and Blossom. By the way, are you two in Saturday's tennis match? Don't overdo in the garden for this week, then. Finish the border and go and sit quietly with your books."

She passed on to see what Madge and Hilda were doing.

"It's this wretched bindweed, Miss Everett," Madge said despairingly. "I'm sure we dug up every single scrap we could see only last Friday and just *look* at it in this corner!"

"I know!" The gardening mistress spoke with fervour. "Once get it into a garden and it takes literally years to clear it out unless you can use weed killer to it."

"Why can't we do that?" Hilda asked hopefully.

"It would mean removing every single plant you wanted to keep. No, thank you, Hilda. We'll leave weed killer alone. Anyhow, you *are* getting the better of it. This part of the garden was nearly swamped in it last year and it's reasonably clear now."

Miss Everett stopped there and looked round, noting which girls were at work. Blossom saw her, and wondered what her expression meant; but Bess Appleton came in search of the mistress just then and she went off to the herb path, leaving the girls working steadily.

Ten minutes later, Katharine stood up and stretched herself with a sigh of relief. "There! I shouldn't think there's a pansy has a hope of seeding for the rest of the week, anyhow."

"Don't you believe it!" Hilary, who was the daughter of a nursery gardener in a very large way and who had helped in the garden ever since she was old enough to carry the weeds in her toy wheelbarrow to the rubbish heap, spoke with conviction. "There'll be a whole lot more to be done tomorrow. By the way, Evvy was right about you two. Leave the garden alone until the match is over. Some of those other lazy blighters can come and help instead. Where are they, by the way?"

"Gwen and her crowd are helping with the goose-gogs," Katharine said. "Megan means to bottle tomorrow. They asked us to join in, but you know what ghastly spikes those bushes have and we thought we'd better not look clawed from here to yonder when Saturday comes!"

"I couldn't agree more," Hilary grinned. "Heaven knows what Campden House might imagine if you turned up on the court with your classic countenances and your arms and legs all scratches! Probably that we settled our differences here with our *nails!*"

"Wouldn't that be nice!" Blossom returned the grin. "Anyhow, we thought picking pansies would be a more suitable occupation. As for Jennifer and the rest, I haven't had a sniff of them since tea-time."

"They loath gardening,' put in Hilda, who had joined them. "I don't believe Jennifer's put in a single evening this term."

"Jennifer's a loathly little slacker!" Hilary picked up her bast and moved on to a delphinium which was shooting skyhigh and in much need of support. "I say, do you think this thing can be descended from Jack's beanstalk? It certainly seems to be aiming at the sky."

"I wouldn't know; but if it isn't tied up, it's going to go *wop!* in the next wind we get," Hilda replied.

"Don't worry. I'm attending to it pronto. Chuck that mallet over as you go out, Kath. I'll have to use one of the big iron stakes."

Katharine obliged, incidentally, nearly braining Hilary with the mallet. Then she and Blossom left the garden to seek books and deck-chairs on the front lawn under the trees. It had been a hot day and even now the sun was blazing, so shade was welcome.

A group of deck-chairs which they passed held the missing Jennifer and the little party she led in Upper Fourth. Katharine went on, but Blossom the impetuous stopped.

"What a set of sickening young slackers you crowd are!" she told them bluntly.

Jennifer looked up from the book she had been reading to the rest. "Well! I like your cheek! Who d'you think you are to come and talk to us like that?"

"Why aren't you in the garden helping?" Blossom demanded. "You never go there by any chance unless it's gardening hour and Evvy's lesson and you've got to. It's jolly rotten of you. You lie back and let other people do all the work and if anyone comes along and admires the place, you stand round smirking with pride as if you'd been responsible for the greater part of it!"

Felicity King and the Wylie twins looked uncomfortable, but Jennifer, who had a hot temper, jumped up. "It's no business of yours! I never asked to be given jobs of that kind and I'm not going to mess up my hands, mucking about with weeds and filthy soil! You mind your own business, Blossom Willoughby, and let us alone!"

"It *is* my business! It's the business of everyone in the form if some of us just laze around admiring ourselves and letting the rest do all the work that belongs to us as a form!" Blossom retorted. "What's more, it's Evvy's business, too. She's just been round and she saw who was working. She generally arrives some time during the evening and unless you take care, she'll begin to notice who's always there and who isn't and make inquiries. *Then* you'll all be for it and serve you jolly well right, too! If you've any sense among you, you'll go and put in a spot of weeding and staking *now*!"

Having fired off this broadside, Blossom strutted off to join Katharine, leaving a fully-roused group behind her. Jennifer was furious and so was Margaret Hart, her boon companion, while the rest were very uneasy at Blossom's final hints about Miss Everett's perspicacity.

Felicity and the Wylies stood up, an example followed rather more slowly by Rosemary Lambe and Angela Wotton.

"Where d'you think you're going?" Jennifer demanded.

"Well, if Evvy's on the prowl, we'd better do something about it,' Felicity said uncomfortably. "She's awfully on the spot, Jenny."

"Oh, rot! It's all the same to her as long as the work gets done. If that conceited young ape, Blossom, and all that crowd like to make a mess of their hands and get backache yanking up weeds and grobbling in the soil, let them! It's just about good enough for them! *I'm* not going to do it, and so I warn you. Don't be asses! Let them get on with it and be hanged to them!"

In her temper, Jennifer stamped her foot as she finished. Her dark eyes were blazing and her cheeks scarlet. The other five looked at her and then at each other. She was by far the strongest character in their little coterie and they were accustomed to following her lead in most things. Blossom's remarks had gone home with one or two of them, however, and they made no attempt to resume their seats.

"It's no go, Jenny," Angela said. "Blossom may be a pig all right, but when she says Evvy's going to take notice because we're never in the garden, she's got it in one. I don't know what anyone else is going to do, but I'm hopping off to do a spot of watering or what-not. Besides," she added cunningly, "it's getting jolly near Madame's birthday. If anyone's in a wholesale row, you

99

know as well as I do she doesn't get a sniff at the expedition. Remember what happened to Vivien James and Marion Orde and Muriel Abbey two years ago?"

Most of those present did, having been Juniors at the time. That hopeful trio had been caught copying a key to their Latin translation a fortnight before the birthday and part of their punishment had been the loss of the expedition to Oxford which had formed the birthday celebration.

This reminder decided the Wylies and Felicity; and Rosemary could usually be relied on to let Angela do her thinking for her. The five moved off in a body, leaving the angry Jennifer alone with Margaret Hart and Sylvia Curling, of whom Hilary had once said, "I suppose they've *something* in their heads—uncooked porridge, probably, or they'd show a little more sense."

"That's Blossom's doing!" Jennifer said furiously. "I'll get even with her, though. Who's she, to talk? She got into rows enough two terms ago. Must have decided to reform and be a little angel," she added with a sneer.

"Oh, let them go," Sylvia returned indolently. "If they like to wear themselves to death, I'm sure *I* don't care! Sit down, Jenny, and forget it and let's go on with the book. It's simply thrilling!"

"Shut up about the book!" Jennifer said sharply.

"No one anywhere near enough to hear," Margaret said. "Come on, Jenny; sit down and let's go on. If those other idiots like to miss it, that's their affair!"

Jennifer allowed herself to be prevailed upon and sat down and picked up the book, carefully shrouded in a brown-paper cover, which they had been reading round among themselves.

All the same, she felt uneasy. *For Ever Amber* is not exactly the type of book any schoolgirl is permitted to read in school—certainly not any schoolgirl of fourteen or fifteen. Jennifer knew this. She had smuggled it in in her hatbox and she knew very well that if any mistress or prefect caught them with it, it would mean a Head's Report. She had found it at home during the holidays and was half-way through it, unknown to her parents, and had brought it back. The others had seen it and wanted to borrow it and they had finally agreed to read round among themselves during their free evening periods.

100

They went on reading, but Jennifer, at any rate, got little pleasure from it. She found herself glancing round every now and then to see if anyone in authority was near. No one came and she was able, when the bell summoned them to the house, to tuck it safely away at the back of her locker.

Nemesis caught up with her next day when Upper Fourth had their regular gardening lesson with Miss Everett.

That lady had promised to teach them disbudding, but before she began, she looked round the form and said blandly, "Hands up, every girl who has not worked in the rock garden this week."

None of the three dared do anything but raise their hands. They knew too well what the rest would say to them afterwards if they did not. Miss Everett nodded as she noted them and also Freda Lund and Amy Dunne.

"You've had a bad hand, Freda, so that's all right," she said. "Is it better yet?"

"Nearly, thank you, Miss Everett."

"What about you, Amy?"

"I was going last night but I had another headache and Matron sent me to bed early," replied Amy, who had been suffering from such headaches off and on for the past two or three weeks.

"Are you all right today?"

"Yes, thank you, Miss Everett. I told Hilary I'd help her finish the staking this evening."

Miss Everett accepted this. Amy was a more or less regular worker and, like Freda, was possessed of a good character. The other three were different and her face froze as she turned to Margaret Hart who was nearest.

"What happened to you, Margaret?"

"I—I—forgot," Margaret said lamely.

"You *forgot*?" There was a nasty little pause. Then, greatly to Margaret's relief, Miss Everett went on to Sylvia. "And may I ask if you forgot, too?"

No reply. Sylvia was lazy and empty-headed, but she was a truthful young person on the whole and knew well enough that forgetfulness was not her reason for neglecting her share of the garden work.

"Gone dumb, have you?" Miss Everett looked at Jennifer. "And am I to take it for granted that you, too, forgot?"

There was an edge to her tone that flicked Jennifer on the raw.

"No, I didn't," she said as insolently as she dared. "I'm just not interested so I didn't go. After all, our free time ought to be our *free* time and I wanted to read."

Now Miss Everett was noted throughout the school for her peppery temper, so the rest of the form gave vent to an audible gasp at this piece of impudence and waited for the mistress to fall on Jennifer with might and main. They were disappointed however, for she did nothing of the kind. Instead, she asked with every appearance of interest, "You don't care for gardening, then?"

"No I don't!"

There was a pause. Then Miss Everett asked gently, "And what was the book you were so anxious to read that you forgot that a certain amount of work in the rock garden during the week is obligatory on every one of you?"

Jennifer stared at her, completely taken aback.

Before she could think of any reply that might pass muster with Miss Everett and yet hide the truth from her, Miss Dene walked into the greenhouse where their lesson was to take place and, if anyone had been interested enough to see it, Miss Everett's face relaxed.

"May Jennifer Penrose go to the study at once, please?" Miss Dene asked.

"Certainly. Go with Miss Dene, Jennifer," the mistress said.

Jennifer turned slowly and followed Miss Dene into the house while the mistress proceeded to rend Margaret and Sylvia to shreds. Sylvia got off with having to spend all her spare time that evening digging up ground elder in the front lawn border with a prefect to supervise her work. Margaret was nearly reduced to tears by the scarification she received for lying, and then presented with a Head's Report so that when the lesson finally began, she got no good of it at all. As for the other five, they blessed Blossom in their hearts for the hints she had dropped the previous evening which had saved them from sharing in the row.

Meanwhile, Jennifer had reached the study to find herself in the presence of both Heads. On the desk before Miss Annersley lay a book she instantly recognised and

102

she shook in her shoes as that lady lifting it asked, "How does this book come to be at the back of your locker, Jennifer?"

Of what occurred thereafter, once she had been brought to owning that she had smuggled the book into school, Jennifer never told even Margaret; but by bed-time, everyone except the Kindergarten knew that she was in deep disgrace.

The birthday festivities were banned to her; she might not mix with the rest until after half-term; finally, and this was what she minded most, she was condemned to doing an hour's weeding in the kitchen garden every week-day, Saturdays included also, until after half-term. She had been in trouble for a similar offence once or twice before, and now she was warned that any repetition of it would mean that her parents would be requested to remove her without further notice. Jennifer's mother was a very easy-going lady on the whole, but the girl stood in wholesome awe of a stern father and she dared not think what would happen if things got to this pitch.

Matron came to remove her to San. when the Heads had finished with her; but first she marched the girl to her dormitory and stood over her while she turned out her drawers, her hatbox and every other hidey-hole she could have had. Another forbidden book came to light and a box of candies which was promptly confiscated to be sent up to the big Sanatorium in the Welsh Mountains. Then she was taken to San., where she was to spend the rest of that day and where she had been told she must sleep for the rest of the half-term.

When Saturday came and she was allowed to go downstairs she found that Margaret, who was smarting under the results of the Head's Report, was sulking with all her might and would not even look at her; and Sylvia, while thankful that she had got off with only a talking-to and a night's weeding in the front garden, also took no notice of her.

As for the other five, Felicity, who possessed the rudiments of a conscience, had given them no peace until they agreed to go with her to the study and own that they had shared in reading *For Ever Amber*.

Since they had owned up for themselves, the worst did not befall them; but the few pointed remarks Miss Annersley addressed to them on the subject went home.

When she told them that they would be sent to other dormitories for the remainder of the term, they felt very subdued and Rosemary began to cry, for this was tantamount to saying that they were not trusted.

Jennifer learnt all this from the conversation of the others, and most unfairly and unreasonably blamed Blossom for it. She was unable to unburden herself to anyone, so brooded over it until she succeeded in persuading herself that Blossom had told tales and Katharine Gordon had backed her up.

"I'll teach them they can't do things like that to me," she thought as she sat at her lonely desk in Big Hall, supposed to be doing her mending. "I'll make them both, and especially Blossom, sorry they behaved like this."

As she sat darning her stockings, she pondered on what she could do and just before the bell rang for Break, a recollection of something she had read years before in a school story gave her what she wanted. The bell rang and she packed up her mending.

"That's what I'll do!" she said to herself as she rolled up the last pair of stockings. "That'll be one for Blossom, anyhow!"

CHAPTER XIII

BLOSSOM IS MISSING

"LOOK at me and for goodness' sake tell me if I look clean and decent!" Katharine spoke agitatedly.

Lunch was always early on match Saturdays to give the girls time to change. At one time people playing in matches had changed first; but since the day that a nervous new Junior had overturned a plate of soup into the lap of Daisy Venables' last clean tennis frock, Matron had ordained that the meal should be earlier and changing come after. That particular affair had been the more trying because Daisy was a long-legged creature, standing five foot nine in her stocking-feet and the frock she had finally managed to borrow from Jocelyn Redford had been a good two inches too short.

When Katharine spoke, standing in the middle of the gangway between the two lines of cubicles, curtains were pushed aside and the seven other occupants of the dormitory in various stages of undress appeared to inspect her.

She wore the Chalet School tennis uniform of sleeveless blouse with pleated shorts. Her long hair was plaited in a pig-tail tied at the end with a flame-coloured ribbon. She was a pleasant-looking creature as she stood there, the sunlight bringing out golden glints in her wavy brown hair, while her tanned face made her eyes almost startlingly blue.

"You look quite respectable," Hilary informed her after taking a comprehensive stare. "Don't forget a clean nose-mat and your blazer—oh, and a pocket-comb in case you need it."

"Wouldn't my sweater be better? I have it here."

"Can if you like; but a blazer's easier to slip into and we aren't allowed to go round with sweaters tied round our necks by the sleeves. Tell you what; give it to me and if you want it it'll be there and you can take your blazer with you."

"I'd tie a band round your head to keep all those ends in," Meg advised. "They may get into your eyes and bother you."

"O.K. Anything else?"

"No, I think not. Any of you others think of anything?" demanded Hilary, not ceasing to brush her curly dark mop as she talked.

No one could; so Katharine handed over her sweater and a couple of extra handkerchiefs to Hilary; accepted Meg's advice and tucked the loose ends waving round her face into a band of flame-coloured ribbon proffered by Hilda Jukes, who always had odds and ends of that sort, and then strolled off downstairs to seek Blossom Willoughby who slept in "Garden" at the other end of the house.

Blossom was nowhere about, so she went directly to the match courts where she found Peggy, Nita, and Natalie Mensch, a slight dark Tirolean, eldest daughter of the school's first Head Girl, who was famed for her steady game and a remarkably tricky service.

"Come along, Katharine," Peggy said encouraginly. "You can come and help to amuse these two while I go off to the drive. Joan being away, I've got to do the polite and welcome the visitors."

Katharine grinned as she dropped down on the seat beside Nita. "I'm glad I'm not you. I should hate to have to go and meet total strangers."

"Oh, it comes with practice," Peggy assured her airily as she departed, passing Daphne Russell and Nancy Chester on the way. Anthea Barnett met her at the rose arch that formed the entrance to the courts and they had a word or two, Anthea glancing down at her watch.

"Young Blossom's taking her time," Nita observed. "Seen anything of her, Katharine?"

Katharine shook her head. "I looked round for her, but she hadn't come down. She's at the other end of the house, you know. Shall I scoot back and tell her to step on the gas a bit?"

"Shouldn't bother. She'll be here shortly," Nancy Chester said, hefting her racquet thoughtfully. "She may be a bit of an ass, but she's nearly crackers with joy at being chosen for reserve, so she won't run it too fine. It's not quite two, yet."

The rest of the school, apart from the Kindergarten who were having a picnic with two of their own mistresses, were now coming in groups of three and four to find places to watch the match.

The Juniors who had been chosen to act as ball-boys formed an excited cluster at the far side of the courts. They made so much noise, that Anthea Barnett frowned and got up to go to them, but Frances Coleman, another of the prefects, had already stopped and was saying something which helped to calm them down, for presently they all sat down at one corner and Frances left them to join Nina Williams, Jean Mackay, and Pamela Whitlock, who were sitting beside the umpire's stand and had saved a seat for her.

Presently Miss Annersley arrived, accompanied by Miss Dene. Miss Burn had gone with the First Eleven and Miss O'Ryan was in charge of the Second; but Mlle de Lachennais and her bosom friend, Mlle Berné, appeared and were surrounded at once by some of the Seniors and Senior Middles, for they were a popular pair.

Miss Slater, the senior Maths mistress, turned up in company with half a dozen of the rest of the Staff, and Hilary and Co. had already made good their claim to the top of the grassy bank above the third court. Blossom had not put in an appearance yet, however, and though she was only a reserve, she ought to have been there by this time.

Anthea leaned forward to address Katharine. "Where's Blossom?"

"I've no idea. Should I go and seek her?"

"Well, it might be a good idea—no, you can't! Here comes Peggy with Campden House. Nita, I'm moving back out of the sun. It's a bit on the strong side today."

Anthea got up and moved her deck-chair back into the shade. She was looking a little pale and shadowy about the eyes, but the team, who were looking anxiously round the chattering groups scattered about, paid no attention to it. Then Peggy, accompanied by a group of white-clad girls, appeared under the roses and was followed by Miss Norman, who was acting Games mistress for today, and another lady with whom she was talking cheerfully.

Katharine felt Nancy nudge her at the sight. "I say, they look jolly strong, don't they?"

"Yes; but that mayn't mean that they're the world's wonders at tennis," retorted Daphne Russell, who had overheard her. "Don't be a little owl, Nance!"

"Come on," said Nita; and, led by her, the team went to meet their opponents and escort them to what had been a large summer-house but was now turned into a dressing-room with running water and pegs round the sides.

Katharine found herself paired off with a pleasant girl of sixteen or so who told her that her name was Mary Martin. Peggy was chatting gaily with a very tall girl, the Campden House Captain, who was called Joyce Lemon; and the rest of the Sixth were "doing the polite" as Peggy had called it, while the visitors laid aside blazers and skirts and changed from sandals into tennis shoes.

Then Miss Norman appeared to ask if they were ready to begin and they went out into the hot sunshine to find that Anthea had distributed the ball-boys, four to each court; Miss Alton and Miss Stephens who, with the Campden House Games mistress, were acting as umpires, were already on their tall seats, with scoring-books and pencils and everything was set to begin.

They had tossed up already, and Katharine had no

time to wonder about Blossom, for Nancy was leading the way to the third court with a big, pretty girl called Valerie and she had to follow with Mary Martin.

Mary had won the toss and chosen service, so that left the Chalet School choice of side. Nancy gave Vi Lucy and Doris Hill a meaning glare as the four parted and those two young hopefuls were on the spot at once with the balls.

"Glad we got side," Nancy murmured to Katharine as they walked across to take up their stances. "We get the advantage of the shade for the first set and when we change round, the sun will have shifted quite a bit and we shan't get it bang in our eyes. Will you take service first or shall I?"

"You!" Katharine said with decision.

"Funker!' Nancy retorted with a grin as she took up her position and crouched at the ready.

Katharine returned the grin but there was no time for more, for Miss Alton had called, "Service!" and already Mary was throwing up her first ball.

It was a long lob and Nancy easily got her racquet to it and sent it flying across the net to Valerie, who took it and returned it to Katharine with a nasty shot that broke out so that Katharine only just managed to get it and return it lamely into the net, and the first point went to Campden House.

Katharine took service next and it came with a force that surprised her. She got to it and sent a return that just skimmed the net. Valerie was ready for it and she drove swiftly to Nancy, who returned it with a clever backhand stroke, taking the other girl unawares, so that if Mary had not raced back, the point would have been lost. As it was, Mary lobbed it over to Katharine who was on her toes now and replied with a really nasty, un-takeable drop-shot and the score stood at fifteen-all.

The game finally went to Campden House by one point and the Juniors were all over the courts, collecting the balls and bringing them to Nancy, who prepared to serve.

There was nothing subtle about her service. She had a good length and the balls were low and swift, but neither Mary nor Valerie seemed to have any trouble in taking them and Campden House won that game, too.

Valerie served next and Katharine, remembering the horrid break she got on her balls, was prepared for anything; so when the service proved to be a long, rather slow lob, she was so startled that she drove it right out of court and the first point of the third game went to Campden House.

Luckily Nancy was roused now, and when Valerie served to her, she took it in the middle of her racquet and returned it with a drive so fierce that it completely beat Mary and the score stood at fifteen-all.

Katharine had recovered herself by this time, and when the ball came, she placed it cleverly just over the net and within the outside line and completely out of Valerie's reach; and when Nancy, driving cleverly to Mary, forced that young lady to return the ball straight ahead, Katharine was waiting at the net for it and smashed it down with the score fifteen-forty.

The final service produced a long rally which ended when the ball broke almost under Valerie's feet and the Chalet School won that game. Hilary and Co., who had been looking very glum, cheered up inordinately and only the courtesy, rigidly enforced on these occasions, prevented them from yelling their heads off.

The fourth game went to Campden House after another long rally, but the Chalet School took the fifth and sixth easily and got the seventh after deuce had been called three times. The score stood at three-four to the Chalet School and Hilary and her crowd sat up and began to take notice.

"I don't think Katharine's playing *quite* so well as usual," Hilary said critically.

"It's playing before a crowd, I expect," Meg replied sagely. "She *is* playing awfully well, though, Hilary."

"Yes; not her absolute best. There's not quite the *bite* in her play. Let's hope she gets down to it now she's got accustomed to an audience," Hilary returned.

Katharine had been saying much the same thing to herself. Mary was a good steady player, but you knew more or less what to expect where she was concerned. If Valerie's balls were allowed to break, they were frequently untakeable. Therefore, Katharine reasoned, they must *not* be allowed to break. She didn't seem able to manage it when she served, however, so that was all right.

Nancy, who had been mopping her hot face, came over while the balls were being collected and spoke to her partner. "Watch that girl's returns," she said with a slight nod towards Valerie, who was re-tying a shoelace. "If we can take 'em on the hop, so to speak, there isn't any real sting to 'em." Katharine nodded as she took the balls from Mary-Lou.

"Go it, Kath!" that young lady admonished her with amazing cheek. "Wipe up the earth with them! You jolly well *can*!"

Katharine chuckled as the blue-eyed Junior scuttled off and tossed up her first ball. She smote it well and truly and it beat Mary completely. Valerie only just managed to return the next and Nancy's backhand sent it skimming over the net to the far corner where Mary got to it, but Katharine, waiting for it, drove it into the inner court to Valerie, who was prepared for a drop-shot which didn't come off. The ball broke in and she never even touched it and the score stood at thirty-love.

Mary was ready for the next, but this time Katharine placed her ball just inside the centre-line and that point also came to the Chalet School. She repeated her tactics with Valerie, who had been prepared for something at the side, drove wildly at it and missed, and they won the first love-game of the set.

After that, Katharine went all out and Nancy after declared that she herself must have been inspired, for she played as she had never played before, even managing the difficult drop-shots which she had worked at unsuccessfully for three weeks, besides strengthening her backhand which was always her strong point. The set ended in a victory for the Chalet School of six games to three. The players straggled up to the net and shook hands, the Campden House girls generously complimenting Nancy and Katharine on the fight they had put up.

"As for you," Valerie told Katharine, "your placing simply had me beat! I never saw anything like it! You seem to be able to put the ball just where you choose."

"Well, I loathed that beastly return of yours," Katharine replied frankly. "It breaks so unexpectedly."

"When it comes off!" Valerie retorted with a chuckle. "It doesn't always, you know. And it's a weird thing, but, try as I will, I never can bring it off in a service."

"That's because you *think* you can't," Mary informed her. "The Bun says that once you realise that you *can* do it, service or otherwise, you will. Let's go and see how the rest are getting on, shall we?"

They strolled across to the court where Peggy and Nita were putting up a good fight against Joyce Lemon and a short dark girl whose service was hair-raisingly swift and had a nasty break on it into the bargain at least three times out of five.

Just as they arrived at the court, it beat Peggy, and Miss Baker, the Campden House Games mistress, called the score: "Forty-love!"

"How do the games stand?" Nancy asked in a swift aside of Bride Bettany, who was sitting near.

"Four-two to them," Bride replied. "They've had some terrific rallies. You people seem to have got through your set fairly quickly. Who won?"

"Us, thank goodness! Katharine played like a demon, especially the last three or four games."

A call of "Service!" stopped the chatter and they turned to watch.

The dark girl, whose name proved to be Marian, served to Nita who got to it with a clever backhand stroke. She must have twisted her racquet as she drove, for the ball broke nastily and Joyce Lemon missed it.

"Forty-fifteen!" Miss Baker called.

Marian served to Peggy, who returned it with a good length shot to Joyce. Joyce drove back to Nita and she sent it down the court with a lightning stroke. It was dead centre and both Joyce and her partner dived for it, with the result that their racquets met in a terrific bang and the ball went flying among the spectators and into the bushes, whence it was retrieved by the chatty Mary Hume at the expense of a scratched nose and a long rip down the front of her frock.

Matron was there, however, and summoned Mary to her promptly to have the rip drawn together, with the result that Mary, as she ever after complained, missed what happened next.

Marian had served to Peggy, who made no mistake about it, but got her racquet well to the ball and drove it across to Joyce. Joyce met it with a short return that just cleared the net and Nita, tearing up the court to take it, slipped, tried to recover, twisted round and fell with her arm doubled under her. She gave a sharp cry and fainted.

111

Play stopped at once, of course. Peggy raced across to her chum who lay white and unconscious near the net. Matron abandoned Mary, leaving her with the needle stuck into her frock, and was speedily beside Nita. Miss Annersley was there now, and so was Miss Baker—the Bun to her unregenerate pupils!—who leaped down from her lofty perch to go to the rescue.

Between them, they lifted Nita gently and carried her to the changing-room. A few minutes later, Miss Norman, who had also gone, came back hurriedly and spoke to Peggy, who stared round the courts and then shook her fair head.

Miss Norman ran back to the changing-room and presently appeared with a megaphone presented to the school by Dickie Christy's father, Commander Christy.

"Blossom Willoughby!" she boomed out. "Blossom Willoughby!"

There was no reply and in five minutes' time it was established that not only was Blossom not there, but that she had never been seen since she had left her dormitory to go down to the courts after changing.

"*Now* what are we going to do?" Miss Norman exclaimed. "Anthea had to go in with a bad headache half an hour ago. She certainly won't be fit to play. Blossom is missing. Who else can we put in as a substitute?"

It certainly was a horrid situation for the Chalet School. Apart from those already in the Six, all the best players were away with the two cricket elevens. Such of the elder girls as were left were good average public school players but no more; and Joyce Lemon and her partner were quite a good deal beyond that standard.

Nancy Chester solved the problem. "Let Katharine play for Nita," she suggested. "She's awfully good and we got through our own set fairly quickly and not too badly, either. I think she could do it."

Miss Norman glanced dubiously at Katharine. "Well—if Campden House agree," she said finally. "I'll ask Miss Baker. And, Nancy, for pity's sake take some of the Middles and hunt through the grounds for Blossom. I can't imagine where she can be and I want to know as soon as possible."

"Yes, Miss Norman."

Nancy paused only to tell Katharine that she must finish the set in Nita's place, since that young lady had wrenched her arm and shoulder very badly and dislocated her collarbone. Then, while the startled Middle turned to pick up her racquet after tossing off her blazer again, Nancy summoned Hilary and Co. from the top of their bank and marched them off for an intensive search of the grounds for Blossom.

CHAPTER XIV

CLYTIE—A STOOL—AND A TENNIS SHOE!

TO go back rather more than an hour and a half. Jennifer, being in deep disgrace, could hardly attend the tennis match. Miss Annersley was by no means strict as a general rule, but there came a point which, if overstepped, meant that the sinner received severe treatment. In passing, it may be said that this had rarely occurred in all the years she had governed the school. Jennifer, however, had decidedly overstepped it on this occasion and the Head had no intention of showing her any indulgence. They had tried gentle means with her, evidently to no purpose: now they must see what severity would do.

The girl had been summoned to the study before Mittagessen and told that she was to take the work Matron would give her after the meal to the rock garden, where she was to stay for the whole afternoon. One of the mistresses would sit with her the first hour and probably Matron herself would come for the rest of the time. At any rate, she would not be left alone because it was clear that she could not be trusted.

Jennifer barely replied. She left the study with a sullen defiant face and the Head wondered, not for the first time, if it would not have been better to cut the Gordian knot and send the girl home at once; but she shrank from doing that. Only twice had the school been forced to go to such lengths throughout its life and she was not anxious to add a third experience of the kind.

Matron's "work" proved to be a sheet to be turned "sides to middle" and, as Jennifer knew, if it were not done to her liking she would order it to be unpicked and done again, so the culprit had an afternoon's hard sewing in front of her. She was fond enough of embroidery, but to sit for a couple of hours or so, working at a long seam, was not her idea of enjoyment.

If it had not been for the trick she meant to play on Blossom, she might even have rebelled openly. As it was, she took the sheet, found her work-basket and carried them to the rock garden, where she found the mistress to be in charge of her had not yet arrived.

"Thank goodness!" she muttered. "If I'm not to be trusted, I'll give them jolly good reason for thinking so!"

She dumped her burdens down on one of the pretty rustic seats and fled round the Kindergarten side of the house.

Ten minutes later, Blossom Willoughby, leaving the house by the side-door always used by the girls, was met by Nancy Chester's small sister, Janice, with a request that she would go to the art room at once as Herr Laubach wanted to see her about her art exam.

Blossom Willoughby was, perhaps, one of the most heedless girls the school had ever numbered among its pupils. She never took time to think that it was most unlikely that the art master would be in school on a Saturday afternoon, but glanced at her watch, saw that the match would not begin for at least another twenty minutes and hurried off to the army hut which formed the art room.

Usually it was kept locked when no work was going on and the key hung on a hook in Miss Dene's office. As it happened, Herr Laubach had been in school that morning to give Anthea Barnett an extra coaching for the scholarship she would sit next week and, finding Miss Dene absent and the study locked, he had left the key in the door. Blossom saw it there, pushed the door open and went in, confidently expecting to see him.

He was not there and she waited a few minutes. Then she decided that he must be somewhere in the other rooms that linked up with the art department by means of a long covered passage. She wandered out, but found them all duly locked, including the outer door at the far end of the passage.

Blossom glanced at her watch again, found that she had been there a good quarter of an hour and decided that she must go.

"I'll have to explain later to him," she thought. "Let's hope I can get up enough German to do it! Anyhow, he's bound to understand when I explain I was reserve for the Six."

She left the art room, shutting the door behind her, and stepped into the little lobby and turned the handle of the outer door. To her dismay the door refused to open. She twisted and pulled, but all to no purpose, for the door remained firmly shut.

For yet another minute or two, Blossom kept calm, thinking that it must have stuck somehow. She called for help, but no help came and when she ceased, the deadly quiet told her that probably every soul in the place was out of hearing by this time.

It must be admitted that she panicked then. She wrenched at the handle until it was a wonder that she did not drag it off. Then she flung open the art room door and rushed to the windows, only to remember with consternation that an attempt at a burglary there during the Christmas holidays had caused the Head to have them nailed up and ventilators inserted in the walls. There were some rather valuable vases and figurines kept in the cupboards for use as models, and the Head was not minded to leave them to any insecurity she could help. Short of smashing a window, and Blossom had not yet reached that pitch, there was no way of getting out.

When she had made up her mind to this, she dropped down on a near-by chair and began to cry. It was quite unlikely that she would be needed, but supposing she were? Whatever would they do? Blossom did not number conceit among her faults, but she knew that her tennis was above the average. She also knew that Joan Sandys had set her heart on their winning this match and if unsentimental Blossom cherished a special feeling for any of the Seniors, it was for the Games prefect. Finally, what *would* everyone think of a reserve who never turned up?

"I've just *got* to get out!" she decided; and went back to make a fresh onslaught on the door.

Nothing she could do made the slightest impression. She twisted the handle; she shook the door; she thumped on it with her clenched fists and finally kicked it as hard as she could. Even this made no difference and as she was in tennis shoes, she only stubbed her toes and the pain forced her to stop.

She tried calling again; but though she shrieked till she was hoarse, no one came, which was hardly surprising. The maids, having prepared tea, were all at the back of the courts, watching the game, and Jennifer Penrose was sitting in the rock garden, sulkily seaming at her sheet. While Miss Bell the handwork mistress, who had volunteered to stay with her for the first hour, lay comfortably in a deck-chair, enjoying her book.

Once more Blossom looked at her watch. It was nearly three o'clock and the match must be well under way by this time. What on earth was she to do?

She went back to the art room and looked hopefully at the ventilators. They were big ones, but not nearly big enough for even her slim form to wriggle through. She turned her gaze on the roof where there were two north skylights set, but they were far beyond her reach, even if she could manage to set a chair on a desk and mount the resultant pile in safety. The army hut was old-style and had been given a steeply pitched roof which soared well beyond any impromptu ladder of that kind.

Calm with the calm of despair, Blossom sat down again, rested her elbows on the desk before her and buried her chin in her clenched fists, thinking hard. What *could* have happened to the door? Such a thing had never occurred before. It would have been all over the school as a good joke if it had! Could someone have turned the key in passing, not knowing she was there? Blossom, like everyone else, knew that the keys were kept in the office as a rule.

"But in that case, what becomes of me?" she said aloud. "Oh, my only sainted aunt! Do I have to stay here till Monday morning? I'll be dead of hunger by that time!"

Tears came again to her eyes at the thought, but she pluckily blinked them away. Then she remembered that if she wasn't missed before, she certainly would be at Prayers. Meantime, *what was happening about the tennis?*

"I'm jolly well getting out *now!* she decided. "I suppose there'll be a most unholy row if I break a window deliberately, but I'll have to chance that. There isn't anything else I can do."

She got up and looked round for something that she could use for the breaking. Apart from desks and chairs and two or three plaster busts on the window sills, there didn't seem to be anything. Anthea, a thoroughly conscientious girl, had cleared up before she left that morning and even the blackboard rulers had been returned to the cupboard where they were supposed to be kept.

"It'll have to be a bust, I suppose," Blossom said aloud. "Let's see: Clytie looks the smallest. Come on, Clytie, my love! You're going to set me free or *else*!"

She had to take both hands to lift the bust, but she managed.

"I'd better use the base. If I smash her precious nose I'll be for it with a vengeance!" she said to herself with a subdued giggle. "Herr Laubach would have forty fits if he didn't die in the first! Anyhow, there'll be row enough about the window, let alone anything else. What's the time now?" She lifted her wrist. "H'm! Half-past three! The sooner I'm out of this the better! Come on, Blossom, my lass! You've got to do it, so stop dithering and get cracking—in *every* sense of the word!" She concluded with another giggle at her own wit.

Then she lifted the bust and banged the base against the lower sash of the nearest window. There was a sharp tinkle and the glass went, most of it outside, but some fell round her. There were still several long spikes left in the frame, however.

Blossom, who had had much ado to save her arms from going after Clytie's base, surveyed them. "I can't get through *those*," she thought disgustedly. "I'd tear my clothes to rags and then *Matey*'d have something to say. I don't think I'll use Clytie again. What about a chair? Or no; that stool over there would be better.

She took the precaution of replacing Clytie on her own window sill, picked up the stool, and holding it so that the seat shielded her face, drove the legs sharply against the remaining glass and cleared most of the sash.

There were still two or three long daggers left. Blossom decided that her shoe would do for them and proceeded to use it with might and main. By the time she had finished, the frame was practically denuded of glass and she decided that she might safely make her escape now.

Pushing her chair up to the window, she knelt on it and then realised that she must clear the sill of glass splinters or she would cut her hands and knees. Her shoe came into play again before she could crawl through, swing her legs out and pull on her shoe again. Then she dropped down, crunching heavily on broken glass and was free at last!

She gave herself a shake, turned and considered the results of her handiwork with a very rueful grin. A sudden shout coming faintly across the match courts recalled her to her duty. She glanced at her watch again. The whole operation had taken much more time than she had thought and it was after four.

"I only hope I've not been needed!" she thought as she set off at her best pace for the courts.

A sound of clapping greeted her as she neared them, and she quickened her steps, anxious to know what had been happening. The applause continued loud and long and, in her anxiety to know how the match was going, Blossom completely forgot that she was filthy, crumpled, her face flushed and tear-stained and her hair a wild sight. She raced down the path, burst through the rose-arch, and saw that everyone was crowded round the centre court and everyone was clapping and cheering enthusiastically.

No one saw her come in and she tore round, seeking a place from which she could see, when she suddenly cannoned violently into someone who caught her with an exclamation.

"*Blossom!* My dear girl, where have you been? And—good Heavens! What *have* you been doing with yourself? Here, come to the changing-room with me at once!"

Blossom looked up. "Oh, Miss Dene! What's been happening? How's the score?"

Rosalie Dene was a good deal more anxious to know what had been happening to the missing reserve, but she replied, "Second pair lost by eight games to five. Third won by three games. First pair have just equalised, thanks to Katharine Gordon who had to take Nita's place when she fell and hurt herself. And now," as they reached the changing-room, "for goodness' sake wash and make yourself as decent as you can, and then tell me what you have been doing."

"But where's Anthea?" Blossom demanded as she turned on the tap.

"Anthea had to go and lie down with a bad head-ache shortly before Nita's accident. Blossom! Tell me where you have been *at once!*"

Thus urged, Blossom told her story as briefly as possible. "One of the K.G. babies came and told me Herr Laubach wanted me in the art room about my exam. next week, so I went there and got locked in somehow. I've been trying to get out ever since." Then she buried her face in the cool water and splashed vigorously.

"Locked in the art room! How could you be? The key's in my office."

Blossom began to dry her face. "No, Miss Dene; it was in the door when I went in."

Rosalie Dene thought back quickly. "Of course! I had to go in to Carnbach this morning and I locked the office before I went. Herr Laubach would have gone before I got back. But how did you get out if the door was locked —and who locked it anyhow?"

"I don't know, Miss Dene." Blossom had finished washing and was combing her thick curls into some sort of order, but she stopped and looked up at Miss Dene with sapphire eyes full of honesty. "I thought at first it was stuck. Then when it wouldn't budge, I knew it was locked and I tried everything else to get out but there wasn't anything, so I—I—" Here she stuck and went scarlet.

"Well—you did what?"

Blossom remained silent. It seemed awful to have to tell Miss Dene that she had smashed a window in cold blood.

"I'm waiting," the lady reminded her.

"Well, you see—I felt I simply *must* get out in case I was wanted, so I—I—smashed a window." Blossom felt relieved, once it was out.

It was Miss Dene's turn to be silent. At length: "You *smashed* a window?" she ejaculated. "How did you do it?"

"Clytie—and a stool—and one of my shoes," Blossom told her succinctly.

"Did you cut yourself at all?"

"No, thank you. Miss Dene, I'm awfully sorry about the window and I'll pay for it, but I simply *had* to get out in case I was needed and it was the only way—Oh, what's that?" for a sudden clapping had arisen.

Miss Dene had been trying to re-set Blossom's pleats. She jumped to her feet and vanished through the doorway, leaving that young woman to contemplate her own reflection in the mirror and decide that she was clean and her hair was tidy, and, short of going to change, there was nothing more she could do.

Miss Dene came back with sparkling eyes. "That was a love game to us on Katharine's service. Are you ready, Blossom? Let me look at you. Yes; you'll pass. It isn't worth while sending you to change now."

"No, Miss Dene. Thank you," Blossom murmured; and prepared to make good her escape.

Miss Dene had not yet finished with her. "Just a moment. The Heads will have to hear this wild yarn of yours, of course, but later will do for that. I won't have anyone from Campden House hearing about it, so don't say anything to the others until after they're gone. If anyone asks what you've been doing just say I know all about it and forbade you to talk of it until after you've seen the Heads. We don't want anyone from another school to get hold of mad tales about us."

"No, we don't, Miss Dene," Blossom agreed with fervour.

"Off you go, then. By the way, don't worry about the window. You had to get free somehow; I see that! And so, I'm certain, will Miss Annersley and Miss Wilson."

"Thanks *awfully*, Miss Dene."

Blossom fled and tacked on to her own chums, Gwen Parry and Elinor Pennell, who welcomed her with grins, but were much too interested in the game to bother about her beyond that. It is true Gwen did ask, "Where on earth have you been?" but a clever stroke from Peggy beat Joyce Lemon completely at that moment, giving the Chalet School yet another game, and in the excitement, Gwen forgot that her question remained unanswered.

As for Blossom, she was thankful to forget all she had been through and concentrate on what was left of the match. It was a hard fight, for every one of the players was on her mettle, and in the final game, deuce was called no fewer than nine times before a drop-shot from Peggy gave them advantage. A minute later, Joyce Lemon caught Katharine's service on the frame of her racquet as the ball broke out, sending it off at right angles, nearly getting Natalie Mensch, who ducked with a wild yell, and catching Mlle Berné on the nose so that her cry mingled with Natalie's shriek. But even Mlle, dabbing with her handkerchief as the blood poured from the smitten organ, forgot about it when Miss Baker called, "Game, set, and match to the Chalet School!" following it up with a hearty, "Congratulations, Chalet School!"

When the opponents had shaken hands and were walking off the court to the changing-room, the Upper Fourth surrounded Katharine, who, they felt, had covered the form with glory, and proceeded to pat her on the back until, as she declared later, she felt like the dog in the game, "The Farmer Wants a Wife."

Blossom was easily one of the most enthusiastic, and Katharine felt herself warming to the girl whose place she had had to take, perforce.

But then, as Peggy Bettany seeing it, remarked afterwards to two or three of her fellow-grandees, that was just Blossom.

"She's a careless imp and even Mary-Lou can't beat her for sauce when she likes, but I will say she's absolutely generous and sporting in the best sense of the word."

CHAPTER XV

CHECKMATE TO JENNIFER!

IT seemed to Miss Dene as if the time would never come when the visitors must leave to catch the ferry back to Carnbach. Until they had gone, she could say nothing about Blossom's experience to anyone, though she had made it her business to go streaking round the house to the art room at the first available moment, in order to survey the window that the young lady had broken.

"My goodness!" she said blankly as she looked at it. "Blossom has been *thorough*—I'll say that for her!"

On her way to have tea with the others, she looked in at the office which was now unlocked, and there hung the art room key on its own hook. She took it down, but it could tell her nothing, so she put it back. By way of precaution, she locked the door when she left the room.

The match had ended at a quarter to five, and after the cheers for each school, Campden House were taken to the very superior Sixth Form splashery, escorted by the prefects who had been playing, while Nancy and Katharine had to fall back on their own forms'.

While she was combing her short thick hair, Joyce Lemon congratulated Peggy on Katharine's play. "How old is she?" she asked.

"Nearly fifteen, I believe," Peggy answered, running a comb through her own silvery-fair curls. "She's quite good for her age, isn't she?"

"My dear, by the time she's our age, she'll be a smashing player in every sense of the word if she goes on as she's doing," Joyce proclaimed solemnly. "Are her people players, too, or is she a kind of sport on the family tree?"

"Her Aunt Luce used to be good, I think. I don't know about her parents. And I say, don't mention them to her, will you?" Peggy said soberly.

Joyce stared. "Why ever not?"

"Because they are the Dr and Mrs Gordon who have been missing so long in China. Mrs Gordon is safe now, I know; but the only news they have of the doctor is fifth- or sixth-hand and it hasn't been confirmed yet, so we can't be sure."

Joyce's eyes widened and emitted a low whistle. "So *that's* who she is! Well, I'm in a position to inform you that it's O.K. about her father. My dad's in Japan and we had a letter from him two days ago—Mother sent it to me and my kid sister to read—and he mentions Dr Gordon and says it's been established that he's been taken to Manchuria to some big hospital there. He's an awfully fine surgeon, you know. I've heard Dad talk of him. I believe they've met two or three times. Look here; I'd better say nothing to the kid herself today. She'll be all revved up anyhow! Especially," she concluded generously, "seeing it was a lot owing to her that you've beaten us out and out."

"Yes; I think that'll be wiser," Peggy said thoughtfully. "She's not a kid that talks much, but I do know that when the news came about her mother she rather collapsed and Matron kept her in San. for a day or so."

"I don't wonder—poor kid!" Joyce considered a moment. "I'll tell you what. Don't say anything, and I'll send you the bit of Dad's letter that mentions Dr Gordon and you can show it to her. Let me have it back as soon as you can, though, as I must return it to Mother."

"Oh, rather! Would you do that, Joyce? That's awfully decent of you. It would buck Katharine up, I know. Ready? Then we'd better move. Tea ought to be ready and I'm sure you could do with it."

They left the splashery, followed by the others who had been too busy chattering to notice them. Tea followed with the usual brief speeches of congratulation on either side. It ended at a quarter to six and as the ferry would not leave until half-past, the Chalet School Seniors took their guests out into the grounds and showed them the gardens.

Jennifer, in San. since five o'clock, had no idea what had been happening. She spent the afternoon alternating between triumph and trepidation. She had locked Blossom Willoughby into the art room, thus preventing her from having any chance of playing in the match, and she could guess just how Blossom felt about it. She intended to take the first opportunity of slipping out and opening the door as she had no wish to start up any hue and cry after the other girl. It never struck her that Blossom was not the type of girl to wait tamely until she was released. All the same, she was a little anxious as to how she was to manage to get the key and unlock the door.

"I ought to have left it where it was," she thought. "But then if anyone had happened to come past and hear Blossom making a hullabaloo, they could have released her at once. Putting it back in its proper place meant that they would have to hunt for Miss Dene to get it, and that wasn't what I meant at all."

Matron, bringing her tea, told her coldly that the school had won, but did not see fit to give her any details, so she imagined that no reserves had been needed and Blossom was still cooling her heels among the desks and models.

When she had finished her tea, she went to sit by the window and saw the others and their visitors strolling about to grounds chatting cheerfully. Matron came to fetch the tray and told her, still in that icy voice, that she might take a book from the bookcase and read till bed-time. Then she went away and Jennifer was left alone.

She went to the bookcase and took out a book—*any* book!—and sat down by the window again; but she only laid it on the sill. Then she tiptoed over to the door, opened it a crack and listened. The only sounds that drifted up came from the kitchens. She went back to the window and saw Matron joining Miss Slater and Miss Stephens. Miss Dene, accompanied by two of the Special Sixth, also went past, and she had seen Miss Annersley leading the way to the rose garden with a stranger who must be the Games mistress from Campden House. The coast ought to be clear now.

She went to the door again and listened. No; there was no one about. Moving carefully, with every nerve on edge, Jennifer slipped down the stairs which, luckily for her, ended opposite the office door, peeped both ways along the passage to make sure no one was coming, and then, taking all her courage in her hands, went on and turned the handle. The door did not give, however, and, with a feeling of bitter disappointment, she realised that Miss Dene must have been in and locked it. The only other entrance was through the study.

Even in her present mood, Jennifer did not dare risk that way. She had no valid reason she could give for being there, and if she were caught, everything was bound to come out. She had triumphed all the way up to now; but now Fate had cried "Halt!" and, so far as she could see, there was nothing she could do about it.

"There's one thing," she muttered to herself as she made the return journey to San., "I don't believe that kid, whoever she was, will have the faintest idea who *I* am. There's a lot to be said for keeping the K.G. babies apart from the rest of the school!"

She reached San. in safety, shut the door, sat down at the window again and picked up her book. She began to read, but it is safe to say that she took in nothing of what she was reading, or she would certainly have flung it down. Indeed, when Matron looked in on her on her way to her own room just before the visitors left, she was startled when she recognised a quaint, old-fashioned story by A.L.O.E., and she wondered what a sophisticated young miss like Jennifer Penrose could be make of *The Crown of Success*!

The same ferry that would bear the Campden House team back to the mainland had brought the Elevens home. Second Eleven were jubilant, for they had beaten Carnbach Grammar by twenty-seven runs. The first had been beaten by one run exactly, but they were not down-hearted. The Sacred Heart First Eleven had a tremendous reputation that season, and, as Joan said, it was no disgrace to be beaten by such a narrow margin, all things considered.

Miss Burn was overjoyed to hear that the Tennis Six had won so handsomely; but she was puzzled when she heard that Katharine had played in Nita's place after the accident.

"Katharine Gordon?" she said. "What on earth was wrong with Anthea and Blossom?"

"Anthea had to go in with a bad headache," Matron, who was her informant, told her. "Nothing to worry about —just the heat. She's never been able to stand much in that way, you know."

"No," Hilary Burn agreed. "I know that. But what about our one and only Blossom? Where was she?"

"I can't tell you. She wasn't there when they called for her, so Miss Norman and Peggy put Katharine in, and I must say she played remarkably well."

"I see." Hilary Burn said no more, but she went to change into less formal garments, feeling that something very odd must have happened. She knew how thrilled Blossom had been when she had been chosen for one of the reserves.

Fuller information came when Miss Annersley sent for the Staff to come to the study and told them Rosalie Dene's story.

"Who on earth was pig enough to play a trick like that on Blossom?" Miss Burn demanded indignantly. "Or was it just that some ultra-conscientious soul passed, saw the key in the lock and turned it and took it away for safety's sake? In that case I must say I wish she'd carried her conscientiousness a little further and looked in to see that the place was empty before she did anything so mad."

Miss Annersley glanced round the assembled mistresses, but one and all disclaimed any responsibility for doing such a thing.

"Perhaps it was Tom Gay," Mlle de Lachennais suggested with an amused smile. "Tom, as some of us well remember, locks doors that seem to her suspicious. Have you forgotten what happened two years ago?"

Such of the Staff as had been in that affair broke into peals of laughter, and the rest sat up alertly and asked what the joke was.

"We'll tell you later on—perhaps!" Miss Wilson replied.

"At present, we have our hands full enough without worrying about bygones."

"What is the time?" Miss Annersley asked. "The clock has stopped and my watch strap broke so I'm not wearing it."

"It's just on seven," her partner informed her. "Shall we let them have Abendessen first and make inquiries then? We should have them all together then."

Miss Annersley concurred in this, but added that she thought they should hear Blossom's story first. Also, she wanted to see the window.

The Staff rose and went out in a body to survey the damage.

"The child might have been seriously cut," the Head said as she saw the broken glass on the ground. She gave a little shudder.

Miss Wilson saw it and promptly administered what comfort came into her head. "Luckily, her guardian angel seems to have seen to that. I must say," she added reflectively, "he must be kept busy. Blossom is the most careless monkey I ever met. She simply sees a thing and does it regardless of consequences. Don't you worry, Hilda! She's come through all right and that's mainly what matters—so far as *she's* concerned."

Miss Annersley gave a rather rueful laugh. "Yes, I know you're right. All the same, I feel rather sick when I think what *might* have happened."

"In the meantime," Miss Burn said briskly, "we can't leave the place like this for anyone to walk in and help themselves to what they like. The locks on those cupboards would be as much use as a sick head-ache to any determined burglar, and it's well away from the bedrooms."

"Yes," the Head agreed. "It must be boarded over until Monday, at any rate. Miss Everett, could you and Miss Bell manage that? The men will all have gone home by this time."

"Oh, yes; we'll see to that," Miss Everett replied. "There are a couple of big boards in one of the toolhouses, so we can nail them over easily."

"Thank you. Then we'll leave that to you two. Miss Dene, would you find someone to send Blossom to the study?"

Miss Dene went off, and the Head turned to the rest.

126

"I think some of you had better join the girls in the garden. We two," she glanced at Miss Wilson, "and Mlle de Lachennais and Miss Burn can hear Blossom's story and see if we can get any help from that, if the rest of you would see to the girls. Abendessen will be at seven-thirty tonight, so they ought to be coming in to tidy up in about ten minutes' time."

The three she had named went with her to the study while the others went to see what the school at large was doing. Matron, who had been up to the Fuchsia dormitory to see how Anthea was and come back to report that she had had a good sleep and the headache was gone, informed the Heads that she had asked the girl if she knew anything about the locking-up of the art room. Anthea had replied that she had not been near it since that morning when she had left Herr Laubach there, busy with his own concerns. Matron had advised her to undress and go to bed properly, and Peggy, who was her room-mate, would bring up her supper.

"Quite right, Matey," Miss Wilson approved. "These headaches of hers always take it out of her. She'll be all right in the morning, I expect. Can't anything be done about them, by the way?"

Matron shook her head. "Jack Maynard overhauled her last summer and he said he was afraid it was constitutional, though she might improve as she grew older. It's only this last three years or so that heat has affected her like this."

"Well, it's a pity, for it spoils such a lot of her summer fun. Yes; I'm coming!"

She turned and left Matron, who was on her way to St Agnes, the Kindergarten House, and joined the others in the study where they sat down round the open window and awaited the arrival of Blossom.

CHAPTER XVI

"WHO DID IT?"

MISS DENE met Katharine as she rounded the corner of the house and told her to go and find Blossom and send her to the study at once.

"Yes, Miss Dene," Katharine replied.

"Do you know where she is?"

"She said something about taking her book to the rock garden. I'll look there first, anyhow."

"Very well—Oh, and tell her to hurry up, please."

"Yes, Miss Dene."

Katharine ran off, and Rosalie Dene returned to the house and joined the party in the study. Katharine found Blossom sprawled in a deck-chair, buried in *Greenmantle*. She made a face when Katharine gave her the message.

"Oh blow, bust, and *bother!*" she commented as she stood up. "Am I decently tidy?"

Katharine inspected her. "As much as ever you are. Blossom, what *did* happen to you this afternoon?"

"Wouldn't you like to know?" Blossom retorted as she made her escape.

Gwen Parry, who had been sitting near, looked up. "She says that Miss Dene knows all about it and said she wasn't to talk to anyone until she had seen the Heads," she explained.

"I suppose that's why they've sent for her, then," Katharine responded, sitting down in Blossom's chair. "Ow! How stiff I am! You know, Gwen, I just don't understand it. Blossom was bucked to the teeth when she was chosen. It's not like her to be missing for that sort of thing, is it?"

"It isn't; but she's been dumber than a starfish about what happened." Gwen closed her book and leaned forward eagerly. "I say, Kath, you might show me how to manage that drop-shot of yours. I've tried all I know to get it, but I simply can't manage it, somehow."

"O.K.; I'll show you. By the way, has anyone heard how Nita is now?"

"Yes; Blossom was allowed to go and see her after tea —they're cousins, you know—and she says Nita's in a good deal of pain but the doctor had been and put the collar-bone back. She's to stay in bed for a day or two, but after that, he thinks she ought to be able to get up. She's not to go to San.—which is just as well, seeing Jennifer's been sent there. She has one of the two-bed dorms with Nina Williams, so there's no need."

"It's jolly hard luck on her! She probably won't be able to play again this summer," Katharine said; and Gwen agreed.

They were still discussing it when the bell rang for Abendessen and they had to go to the house.

For once, there would be no dancing afterwards. They had already been told that after the meal they could go back to the garden until bedtime. All who had been playing in matches that day were tired enough to be glad of this; the rest had no objections to being free to go their own ways for once.

The Kindergarten were all in bed by this time, but everyone else was in the dining-room with the exceptions of the two invalids and, of course, Jennifer, to whom Matron had taken a tray earlier. Blossom, seated in her usual place between Bride Bettany and Julie Lucy, did not look unduly upset, though several people demanded to know what had happened to her during the afternoon.

"You'll know all in good time," she told Polly Winterton airily. " 'Twasn't *my* fault, anyhow, and the Heads know."

"Oh, let the little ass alone!" Tom Gay exclaimed as Polly opened her mouth to press the question. "It'll be something idiotic, or I don't know young Blossom!"

Bride was quick to pick up her friend's cue. "What did you think of that demon bowler?" she asked conversationally. "Personally, I call the girl a menace! Her balls come down like torpedoes. When I saw the first one coming, I felt like getting behind the wicket and shrieking for help! I never met a girl who bowled like that before."

Thereafter, the conversation at their table dealt strictly with cricket and Blossom was left to eat her meal in peace.

When Abendessen finished, Miss Annersley rose to say Grace. Before she did so, she said, "When Grace is ended, all sit down again, please. I have something to say to you."

A good many meaning looks were directed at Blossom; but though that young lady flushed, she contrived to look as nonchalant as ever. They stood for Grace and then sat down, everyone turning to look up the long room at the Head, who had remained standing. Matron, sitting near the top door, had slipped out unnoticed when Grace finished and the Head said nothing until she returned with Jennifer, who was directed to an empty seat at the end of the Staff table.

Miss Annersley went straight to the point. "This afternoon, a few minutes before the tennis match began, little

Janice Chester brought Blossom Willoughby a message purporting to come from Herr Laubach and telling her to go to him in the art room. She went. If she had taken time to reflect, I think she would have realised that Herr Laubach was most unlikely to be in school on a Saturday afternoon. As it was, she promptly rushed off and, thanks in part to her own heedlessness, spent a most unpleasant two hours or so there. Someone locked her in and she was unable to get out normally, so she broke one of the windows and climbed out that way."

Jennifer was unable to restrain a gasp at this. She had never dreamed that Blossom would go to such lengths. However, most of the others gasped, too, so it passed unnoticed.

"And now," Miss Annersley said, "I want to know who did the locking-in and who sent that message?"

There was silence while the girls looked at each other. Blossom, thus publicly rebuked, sat with scarlet face and wished it was in order for her to disappear under the table. She had not been spared in the study, for it had been pointed out to her very plainly that her own lack of thought had been largely to blame for her unpleasant experience, so she thought the Head might have spared her now.

The silence continued, so Miss Wilson took up the tale. "If anyone locked that door for a silly joke, own up at once and don't be silly," she said brusquely. "We know it was none of ourselves nor the kitchen staff, so it *must* have been one of you."

Still no response, though Jennifer wondered if it would be better if she said she had seen the key in the door in passing and had turned it. Then she remembered that the Head evidently knew that Janice had brought a message so it *must* have been a put-up job. She decided to hold her tongue and hope that the small girl would be unable to say which girl had given her the message.

Miss Annersley spoke again. "Does anyone know anything about it? I warn you, girls," she added very gravely, "that we intend to get to the bottom of this. I don't know if you realised that Blossom might have been seriously hurt when she broke the window. If anyone knows anything about it, please own up at once. It will be far worse for you if you leave us to find it out for ourselves."

Peggy Bettany answered for the others when she stood

up and said, "I don't think any of us *do* know, Miss Annersley."

The faces of the two Heads became very grim and, for reasons that she could not fathom, Jennifer suddenly turned chilly.

Peggy sat down again when she had spoken and Miss Annersley, standing very straight, said coldly, "Then it seems we have a coward in this school. I am sorry, girls, but I am afraid we can't accept Peggy's assurance in the circumstances. We must find out just where each one of you was between two and two-fifteen which is when the trick must have been played."

Miss Burn leaned forward and spoke urgently for a minute. The Head nodded and turned again to the girls.

"Miss Burn reminds me that none of the cricket elevens could have had a hand in the matter as they left for the mainland by the ten-thirty ferry. Those girls may go to the gardens. Please amuse yourselves quietly."

The teams, with their reserves and the friends who had gone with them, rose and left the room, full of curiosity but not daring to stay. Only once before had any of them seen Miss Annersley look so stern and there had been serious trouble then.

The Head waited until the last girl closed the door behind her. Then she returned to the matter in hand. "Peggy, what time did you go down to the tennis courts and was anyone with you?"

"Nita, Natalie and I went down together at ten to two," Peggy said. "Katharine Gordon came along a minute later and then I went to the drive to be ready to welcome Campden House. I passed Daphne and Nancy on the way and Anthea was just behind them."

"I met Peggy on the drive at five to two," Miss Norman said. "I remember looking at my watch and saying we were in plenty of time."

"Did either of you three go back to the house for anything?" Miss Annersley asked. "Or you, Daphne and Nancy?"

"No, Miss Annersley." It came in a chorus.

"Then I think we can exonerate you. You may go."

They departed, to be seized on by the cricketers as soon as they reached the garden, and severely interrogated as to what had been happening, but none of them could tell much, and half-way through what they *had* to tell, one of

131

the maids came to fetch Katharine to the office where she was wanted on the telephone.

Meanwhile, the two Heads, with some help from the Staff, questioned the girls as to when they had gone down to the courts, and where they had been just previously. They got through fairly quickly, for most of the girls had been with friends and they had gone down in threes and fours and never been alone all the afternoon. As they were proved blameless, they were sent out until finally only four were left—Mary-Lou Trelawney, Viola Lucy, Jennifer Penrose, and Blossom herself.

Mary-Lou explained that she had lost the ribbon from one of her pigtails and had had to run back to find another. Luckily for her, Matron had met her and had plaited up the loose hair again for her, so she was sent off.

"What about you, Viola?" Miss Wilson said.

Viola looked scared at the sound of her full name which was rarely used. "I met my cousin Janice," she replied, "and she wanted me to have one of her sweets so I took one. That was all. I met Mary-Lou when Janice ran because Miss Morley was calling her, and we went down to the court together. We were being ball-boys," she added importantly.

Miss Annersley bit her lips to hide a smile.. "Very well, Vi," she said. "You may run along now."

Vi, thankful to hear the usual shortened form of her name, gave the Head a dazzling smile and departed. Only Jennifer was left to question now.

Miss Wilson looked at the girl curiously. Surely *she* could have had nothing to do with it. She had been in charge of a mistress the whole afternoon. It seemed impossible that she could have had a hand in it.

Miss Annersley looked down the long table at her. "Come here, Jennifer," she said, pointing to the opposite side of the table.

Jennifer came slowly and stood staring up at the tall Head with sullen eyes. She was determined not to admit she knew anything about it—yet; but she had had some experience of both Heads and knew it would take all her determination not to confess.

Miss Annersley looked straight down into the black eyes as she asked her question. "Had you anything—anything whatsoever to do with locking Blossom into the art room?"

132

Jennifer had stared up into the Head's face at first, but now her eyes dropped and she muttered, "I don't know what you are talking about."

"That is not true, Jennifer." And oh, the ice in Miss Annersley's beautiful voice! "You were present when I told the rest just now, and are you going to tell me that you deliberately became deaf to what I was saying?"

As that was much more than Jennifer dared venture, she made no reply to this. Her gaze roved uneasily round and finally came to rest on her own interlocked fingers on the edge of the table.

"Answer me!" Blossom literally jumped at the tone in the Head's voice. "Look at me while you speak and tell me the truth. Did you lock Blossom Willoughby into the art room this afternoon?"

Jennifer summoned up every ounce of courage and will-power she possessed and looked straight into the icy blue-grey eyes fronting her as she said, "No; I didn't. I was in the rock garden. Miss Bell was with me the first part of the afternoon and then Miss Andrews took her place until Matron came and sent me upstairs to San."

It was the custom of the Chalet School to accept the word of any girl unless it was proved that she was lying. Miss Annersley asked no further questions. She simply replied, "Very well. You may go back to San. Matron, will you take her up, please."

Matron went to the door and Jennifer reluctantly followed her from the room. The Head turned to Blossom, who was fidgeting uncomfortably.

"You may go now, Blossom. Another time, please try to keep your head and *think*!" I'll see Janice in the morning and find out if she knows who it was that gave her the message."

"Yes, Miss Annersley. Thank you."

Blossom made her escape thankfully, and the Head, turning to the rest, made a gesture of despair. "Someone definitely did it. The lock couldn't have slipped of itself and the key was certainly on its proper hook when you looked, Miss Dene—Why," as she suddenly realised that Rosalie was not there, "where has Miss Dene gone?"

"Olwen called her out of the room while you were questioning the girls," Miss Wilson said.

"It was a telephone call," Biddy O'Ryan put in.

"Something important, if Olwen's face was anything to go by."

Miss Annersley nodded and turned to the others again. "Do you realise that this means that someone is deliberately lying?"

"Then someone's being a complete idiot!" This was Hilary Burn, "Apart from anything you two may decide on as a punishment, her own little pals will have quite a lot to say when it *is* found out. I wouldn't be in *her* shoes for all the tea in China!"

"Do you think it could be that new monkey, Norah Fitzgerald?" Miss Stephens demanded. "She came here with a sweet record for mischief, so I'm told."

Miss Wilson shook her head. "Her father told me that she was a young demon, but he could say that she had never told a lie in her life, not even when she knew the truth meant heavy punishment. So far as I know she's been truthful enough while here?"

She glanced across at Miss Bell, who was the young lady's form mistress. Miss Bell nodded vigorously.

"She's a demon all right, and her sins are rapidly turning my hair grey, but she's absolutely truthful. You let her alone, Stephens, and think of someone more likely."

"Oh, well, it was only an idea," Miss Stephens murmured.

"A jolly rotten one, then!" Miss Bell might suffer from the monkey-tricks of Upper Third, but she stood up for them with might and main whenever it was possible.

"Stop it, you two!" Miss Wilson spoke forcibly. "We've enough on our hands without any argy-bargying."

"Could it have been Miss Denny?" suggested Hilary Burn. "She told me she was going to Armiford for the week-end. D'you think she turned the key on her way to the Christys? She told me Commander Christy was running her across in his motor-launch."

Miss Annersley shook her head. "Quite impossible. Commander Christy rang up this morning to say he found he had to leave an hour earlier than he intended and to ask her to be at their place by eleven."

"Besides," added Miss Wilson, "there was that message Janice brought. No; I'm afraid we can wash out any idea of accident. This was done in malice and to stop Blossom having any chance of playing in the match."

"And that," Miss Annersley said, "is what seems to me almost the worst part of the whole thing."

"Then," Hilary voiced the question that was bothering all of them, "*who* did it?"

There was no chance for anyone to reply to that, for at that moment Rosalie Dene burst into the room with a face full of excitement. "Miss Annersley," she cried, "that was Miss Gordon on the 'phone. She's in England—in London actually—and she's coming here first thing on Monday to see you. She was most fearfully apologetic and she says she must see you as soon as possible."

Miss Annersley subsided into her chair with a groan. "What on earth is going to happen next?" she ejaculated.

"I don't quite know, but I have an idea that she's coming to explain the mix-up about Katharine. She was appallingly incoherent, but I gathered there had been some muddle over a letter or letters. However," Rosalie concluded, "we shall know on Monday. I only hope she means to leave the kid here. We don't often get a girl who is obviously headed for Wimbledon as soon as she's old enough, and we can do with her!"

"We can indeed." Hilary fully agreed with this dictum. "But *will* Miss Gordon have the say-so? Isn't Katharine's mother supposed to be coming to England shortly? There you are then. It's she you'll have to get hold of. I couldn't agree more, of course. We must hang on to Katharine if it's at all possible."

"We have the vacancy at present," Miss Dene said. "The thing is, shall we have it for next term? I know a number of Seniors are either leaving or going to Switzerland for their final year. At the same time, we've booked a good many new girls for next term—including Mary-Katharine, who will, I suppose, be coming then, at any rate. Sybil Russell and Josette will be back we expect, not to speak of Jo's trio. This place will be chock-a-block."

"What about Plas Howell? Won't it be all right by that time?" Hilary turned to the Heads.

"We hope so," Miss Wilson agreed. "At the same time, there is still quite a good deal to be done and we may not be able to move back until after the half-term. We shall know better at the end of this term." Then she added wickedly, "In any case, I hardly see that it will matter to you. Correct me if I'm wrong, but aren't you marrying that nice doctor-man of yours in August?" .

Miss Burn went darkly red, much to the delight of the younger members of the Staff, but she retorted, "I am! When I found I was to be ousted from my position as Staff baby, I decided it was time to make a move. But that needn't prevent me from being keen to keep a girl in the school who is likely to cast a few laurels at it."

Miss Wilson stood up and pulled up her co-Head. "Come along, my dear. You look very much the worse for wear, thanks to all this sickening business, and much too tired to bother about Hilary's matrimonial plans. You go to the rose-garden with some of the others and she and Rosalie and I will make coffee and bring it out there. I think we all need something in the way of a stimulant after all this!"

CHAPTER XVII

AUNT LUCE DOES IT AGAIN!

SUNDAY brought them no nearer a solution of the problem. All small Janice Chester could say when questioned by Miss Annersley was, "It was a girl with *very* dark hair—I know that. But I don't know her name. You see," sedately, "St Agnes' House doesn't 'sociate much with the rest of the school."

Miss Annersley bit her lips as she looked at the small girl standing before her, serious little face, with its frame of waveless black hair and the beautiful Irish grey eyes she had inherited from her mother, raised gravely to the Head.

"Very well," she said. "If you can't remember, you can't. But Janice, if you see her, come and point her out to me. It's rather important. One thing more: I want you to give me your promise that you won't talk about this to the others. Will you?"

"Oh, yes; I promise, of course," Janice said.

She trotted off after that and the Head was left to wish that Joey Maynard was somewhere near at hand instead of being well over three thousand miles away.

"I do *miss* Jo!' thought the worried lady. "She can generally get down to the bottom of things, and even if she can't, she can suggest some sort of solution to most problems."

She had a good deal to trouble her that day. Nita, never a very strong girl, had had a bad night with a very high temperature owing to the pain she was enduring. That dropped a little before morning, but she was still ill enough to be a source of anxiety to the Heads and Matron, who wanted to keep the story of her accident from her parents as long as possible. Mrs Eltringham had remained frail after a bad attack of pleuro-pneumonia three years before and this had meant extra help at the Vicarage, for there were five boys between Nita and the four-year-old Rosamund, who was the baby of the family. The Vicar himself was a busy man with a large and scattered country parish, and money was far from being plentiful, so that unnecessary journeys were out of the question.

As if that, added to the Blossom mystery, were not enough for anyone, Matron had been in early that morning to report that Jennifer Penrose had had one bad bout of nightmare after another throughout the night and was really poorly this morning.

"I can't think what's wrong with her," Matron said anxiously. "I *know* she had nothing for supper to upset her and she's not given to nightmare as a rule. She's certainly not herself this morning."

"I don't want her kept in bed unless you must," Miss Annersley replied. "It's hot already and will be hotter later on. I think you had better send her to the rose-garden for the day."

The rose-garden was the favourite stamping-ground of the Staff during the evenings and the week-ends, so certainly Jennifer would not be able to talk to the other girls if she were there. It was decided that this was the best thing to do with her and the Staff had to put up with it.

There was no question of moving Nita. She must remain in bed until her temperature came down. Nina Williams had been moved into Jennifer's vacant bed so that Nita might be alone for the present, and that had meant extra trouble. Altogether it was a very trying Sunday and Anthea Barnett topped it off by fainting in church in the evening. Miss Annersley felt thankful when bedtime came and no other trouble had arisen.

Monday morning brought better news all round. The pain was subsiding in Nita's arm and shoulder and her temperature had dropped in consequence. She was still unable to move without crying out and she complained of a dull toothache pain all over, but the doctor, when he came, said that she was definitely better and should be up and about by the end of the week.

Jennifer, too, had slept better, though her eyes still looked heavy and she was rather white. She had relapsed into a sulky silence, but as that was her usual reaction to any punishment, no one thought anything of it.

Work went on as usual and Miss Annersley, who taught most of Monday morning, found quite enough to do to keep her from thinking about external problems.

She had literature with Upper Fifth first lesson and then English with Upper Fourth at the other end of the house. On the way there, she had to pass Upper Third and, to her amazement, found Mary-Lou cooling her heels in the corridor.

"What are you doing here?" she demanded.

Mary-Lou turned very red. "Miss Edwardes sent me out of arithmetic," she stammered.

"Why?" the Head demanded severely.

"Well, I—I wasn't—behaving."

Miss Annersley looked her up and down without a word and Mary-Lou's fair head sank until it could go no further.

"Go to the study and wait there for me," the Head commanded at last; and Mary-Lou went, laggingly.

Miss Annersley hurried to the Upper Fourth, where she set them to work on a piece of paraphrasing nicely calculated to keep them occupied for at least twenty minutes, and then went to the study to interview the culprit.

It took her exactly five minutes to find out that Miss Edwardes, catching the young lady in the act of tilting her chair backwards, a thing forbidden since, in earlier days, one or two girls had had nasty knocks as a result, had said sharply, "Stop tilting your chair backwards!"

"And so," Mary-Lou concluded very shamefacedly, "I did. But then I—I tilted—er—sideways."

"You did *what*?" Miss Annersley ejaculated, scarcely believing her ears.

"I tilted sideways."

"Then you were a very naughty little girl!" the Head

said. "Not very straight, either, for you knew quite well that Miss Edwardes meant that you were not to tilt your chair at all. I am not surprised that she sent you out of the room. You will apologise to her for being so disobedient and, since you don't seem to be able to use a chair properly, you may do without one for the rest of the morning."

Mary-Lou's face fell. "Please, we have composition third lesson," she said deprecatingly.

"You should have thought of that sooner. When you have been given your subject, you will take your work to the office and do it at the high desk there—standing. And please let me hear no complaints about bad writing! Now you may go back to your form-room and tell Miss Edwardes what I have said. If she allows you to stay, you do your work standing. Perhaps that will teach you not to tilt in future!"

Miss Annersley stood up and a completely deflated Mary-Lou bobbed her curtsy and crept from the study.

The Head was about to go to her work when Miss Dene appeared, escorting a small slim person with cloudy grey hair wildly tossed by the breeze that had arisen that morning.

"This is Miss Gordon to see you, Miss Annersley," she said formally.

The Head rose with outstretched hand. "I'm so glad to meet you at last, Miss Gordon. Come in and sit down." She glanced at Rosalie. "Will you hurry up the coffee, please, Miss Dene?"

"Yes, Miss Annersley." Miss Dene vanished and the Head was left alone with her visitor.

"I've come to make a confession," Aunt Luce said in much the same deprecating tones that Mary-Lou had used a few minutes since.

Miss Annersley smiled. "Nothing very serious, I expect. Before anything else, may I say how very glad I am to hear of your sister-in-law's safety?"

"Oh, it's my brother, too. That's one reason why I came," Aunt Luce explained as she rummaged in the big canvas bag she was carrying. "When I got to England, I went to the bank and found a whole bunch of letters waiting there. One was from him and it says that he's safe in Chunchow where he was taken a few weeks ago."

By this time, she had found what she wanted, and was

holding out a sheaf of badly crumpled papers. Miss Annersley took them with a feeling of perplexity. Then she saw that one was the Chalet School prospectus and another a letter addressed to the school. Yet a third bore Miss Wilson's name. She stared at them in bewilderment; but Aunt Luce was pouring out her explanation at railroad speed.

"You see, it was this way. My sister-in-law always wanted Katharine to go to the school where the Head or some other mistress was an old schoolfellow of hers. She told me it was the Chalet School, but she didn't have time to give me any details. She was writing when they were arrested and I don't know how the letter got posted. Anyhow, I went to an agency and got the addresses of all the Chalet Schools I could, but only this and one other were any use. The other was in a place called—oh, may I have my papers back, please? I forget the name."

"It is Tanswick, a seaside town not far from here," Miss Annersley replied. "Here comes our coffee. Thank you, Miss Dene," as that young lady set the tray down and then left them again.

The Head poured out the coffee, saw Aunt Luce supplied with cream, sugar, and chocolate biscuits, and then leaned back in her chair, sipping her own cup.

"Well, so you see," Aunt Luce said, "I wrote to both of you. Then, when I'd had the prospectuses, I chose one and wrote to say I was sending Katharine."

Miss Annersley set down her cup. "It was not the Tanswick one, Miss Gordon. When we found that Katharine was *not* entered here, I rang up Tanswick and they told us the only pupil there called Gordon had been with them some years and they knew nothing about any other. We were unable to contact you, so we could only keep her with us until we heard from you."

"Oh, I know!" Aunt Luce burst out. "That's just it! You see, I *wrote* the letter—but I never posted it!"

Miss Annersley was dumbfounded. She was not very sure what to say, so she said nothing and Aunt Luce continued.

"I *thought* I'd posted it, but what with one thing and another, I must have just shoved it into my raincoat pocket and forgotten about it. It was an awfully *old* raincoat and I bought another and put that one away into a cupboard. Then, when I came home after getting your letter at Palmas, I was hunting for something in that cupboard and found my raincoat. I felt in the pockets to see if there were any handkerchiefs or anything else there and found—those!" She pointed dramatically at the crumpled sheaf on Miss Annersley's desk. "I was horrified when I saw them. Of course, I knew something must have happened when I compared the addresses, so I decided to come at once. Anyhow, I wanted to see Katharine and tell her it was all right about her father."

"Then—do you mind telling me if the Tanswick school was the one Mrs Gordon meant for Katharine?"

"Yes; but there was a letter from her, too, telling me that her friend, Miss Wilson, had given up teaching and gone to join a brother in Kenya. So now," Aunt Luce concluded, "I simply don't know *what* to do!"

"Isn't your sister-in-law returning to England shortly?" the Head suggested. "I think your best plan is to leave Katharine here with us until she arrives and then we can see what she thinks."

Aunt Luce looked profoundly relieved. "Oh, if you can keep her I should be really thankful. From her letters, she is very happy here. I quite expect Mary will want her to stay if you can keep her. Can you?"

"I think we can manage to make room for her," Miss Annersley smiled. "Now there goes the bell for Break, so I will send Katharine to you and you can have a chat. No one will disturb you here. By the way, where are you staying?"

"I have a room at the Pembroke Arms at Carnbach. I got there last night and crossed by the ten o'clock ferry this morning."

"Then I hope you will stay for lunch and tea and give Katharine a chance to show you her school."

"Oh, thank you—if it won't be putting you to any inconvenience?"

"Of course not. I'll go now and send Katharine."

Miss Annersley had just reached the door when the visitor spoke again. "I'm dreadfully sorry and I do hope you'll forgive me. It's the sort of thing I'm always doing. I never *mean* to be absent-minded, but I get an idea for a study, or I see a view I simply *must* paint and then I forget everything else. Of course, I did see that other school; but when I saw your girls and their really artistic uniform, I knew this was the school for Katharine."

Miss Annersley made no reply; she was beyond it. She did manage to get safely out of the room, grab Hilary Wilson who was passing, and send her to tell Katharine to go to her aunt in the study. Then she fled along to the Staff room, bursting in on the four or five mistresses already assembled there and giving them all reason for alarm when she dropped into the nearest chair and laughed until the tears poured down her cheeks.

"What's wrong with you?" Miss Wilson demanded in consternation. "Hilda! Stop it, you mad creature! You'll be having hysterics if you go on like this!"

But Miss Annersley was well away and it was some minutes before she managed to control herself sufficiently to explain.

Before she was half-way through, the Staff were laughing as consumedly as she had done, and Hilary Burn expressed the feelings of all present when she choked between wild shrieks of mirth. "Well, I should say that, as Katharine remarked to me once before, 'Aunt Luce has done it again!'"

CHAPTER XVIII

JENNIFER CAVES IN

TUESDAY of that week was known for the rest of the term as "the day of happenings."

It began with Miss Annersley receiving a letter from Jo Maynard among her mail. Jo, as may have been gathered, possessed the pen of a more than ready writer. She also had a habit of letting off bombshells in the middle of a recipe for a cake or the measurements for a tray-cloth. As a result, most of her correspondents were apt to treat effusions with caution.

Miss Annersley was no exception to the rule. She turned the letter over as she remarked to Rosalie Dene who was with her, "I wonder just what shock Jo has in store for me?"

"It needn't contain one at all," her secretary told her bracingly. "The last two you had from her were quite ordinary rhapsodies on the scenery and atmosphere. At least," she added, "Jo's choice of language is never exactly ordinary, but you know what I mean."

"I know; and that's just why I'm expecting something startling this time. As a matter of fact, I didn't expect anything at all from her, seeing I haven't had time to answer those two."

"I should open it and get the worst over."

Thus urged, the Head opened the letter and drew forth a single sheet. "And that's a shock in itself," she remarked pensively. "Jo's screed rarely runs to less than six or seven pages."

"What does she want?"

Miss Annersley quickly scanned the contents and then passed it over. "Here you are. It's your business almost as much as mine."

Rosalie read it, her face growing very grave.

"Dearest Hilda," it ran, "Just a line to say I hope you weren't really reckoning on Mary-Kate Gordon joining you, for she won't. News has come that her father died of typhus a month ago and her mother feels she can't part with her now. Just what they will do, I don't know. I'll write later if I hear anything and tell you. Much love, Jo.

"*P.S.*—I hope to goodness Katharine Mary's folks are safe?"

Rosalie laid the sheet down, looking very sober. "The poor souls!"

The Head was looking very troubled. "It makes me very anxious for Katharine's father. Clearly he has been sent to this new job by the Chinese government. I've heard that typhus is rampant out there and if he's worked to death as I've little doubt he is, he won't stand any better chance than his namesake."

The door opened and Miss Wilson came into the room in time to hear this. "What are you talking about?" she demanded.

For reply, Miss Annersley handed her Jo's letter and she skimmed rapidly through it. Her face was very serious as she finished, for she, too, saw the risk for the other Dr Gordon.

"We can't do anything but pray," she said as she folded

up the sheet. "You won't say anything to Katharine, will you?"

Of course not. She doesn't even know Mary-Kate and they are no relation."

"Not so far as we know," Rosalie amended. "Miss Gordon might be able to tell us. She's still in Carnbach, isn't she?"

"Yes! she said she would stay there over half-term and have Katharine with her instead of letting her go with the North Wales trip. That's an idea, Rosalie. You might ring her up and find out."

Miss Dene nodded and left the room. The two Heads discussed the news until she returned to say that Miss Gordon was not sure, but she thought Mary-Kate's father was a distant cousin. She begged them to keep the news from Katharine.

"I hope you assured her that we would?" Miss Wilson said.

"Yes; I said you felt she ought to know nothing about it."

"Thank you. One can always rely on you to show common sense, my dear—yes; come in!"

Hilary Wilson entered, bobbed her curtsy and announced, "Please, Matron says would one of you go to the San. She wants to see you at once."

"Which of us?" Miss Wilson demanded.

"She didn't say."

"Very well. Thank you, Hilary. You can run along."

Hilary departed and Miss Annersley turned to the other two with a dismayed look. "What's happened *now*? Nell, I think *you'd* better deal with this. You're free just now, aren't you? I'm due with Upper Fifth in ten minutes' time—no, less than five, now," as she glanced at her watch.

"I'll go." Miss Wilson got up and went off upstairs, leaving her partner to give Rosalie Dene a few instructions before she gathered up her books and left the room as the bell went for the end of third lesson.

Matron met Miss Wilson at the head of the stairs leading to San. "Thank goodness you've come!" she said. "As I expect you know, Jennifer had another night of nightmares so I kept her in bed this morning. When I took her elevenses just now, I found her crying and she's done nothing *but* cry ever since. *I* can't get any sense out of her, so I thought one of you had better come and see what you could do. She mustn't be allowed to go on like this, or we shall have her ill with a nervous breakdown on our hands."

"She hasn't had any letters—no; of course she hasn't! Old Griffiths was later than ever this morning and the letters haven't been distributed yet. It can't be any home trouble, then. All right, Matey; I'll see to it."

Miss Wilson strode down the corridor to San. with the long loping step that had made saucy Jo Maynard once liken her to an Alsatian dog, much to her indignation. She went in quietly. Jennifer was lying in the bed nearest the far window. Her face was buried in the pillow and her whole frame was shaking with the violence of her sobs.

The mistress went over to the washstand, took up the sponge lying there and dipped it into the ewer. Then she stalked across to the bed with it and spoke sharply. "Jennifer—*Jennifer*! Turn over at once!"

Very few girls ever cared to disobey Miss Wilson when she spoke like that and Jennifer was not one of them. She rolled over, showing a face so swollen with crying, that Miss Wilson felt a sudden pang of pity for the girl. The next moment, however, Jennifer was gasping, for the mistress was sponging her face vigorously, and the sudden shock of the cold water stopped the tears for a moment.

"Sit up, Jennifer!" she said not ungently, but still firmly. "I'm going to bring you a bowl of water and you are to bathe your face and stop crying at once. Whatever is wrong, crying won't help and you are only making yourself ill."

Jennifer flopped back on her pillow again. "O-oh—o-oh!" she sobbed. "I can't get it out of my head!"

"Can't get *what* out of your head?"

"The blood—the awful blood pouring everywhere!"

For one moment, Miss Wilson wondered if the girl could be delirious; but though she was hot, it was not the dry heat of fever, but the damp hotness that comes from lengthy crying. However, she abandoned the face-washing idea for the moment and sat down on the side of the bed.

"What are you talking about?" she demanded.

"B-Blossom! Cut everywhere! Her f-face s-spoiled!"

"*What*?"

Jennifer was off again, so the mistress got up and left

145

her to it for the moment. Going out of the room, she called Matron, who was hovering anxiously about in the passage.

"Look here, get someone to send Blossom Willoughby up here at once, will you?" she said urgently. "Say I want her and she's to come *now*—without any delay. *She* seems to be at the bottom of Jennifer's attack, so she can deal with it. Thank Heaven, she's as matter-of-fact as they come! Go on, Matey! Find someone and send her at once!"

"I'll go myself!" Matron bounded off and was fortunate enough to find Blossom delivering Upper Fourth's geometry prep for Miss Slater in the Staff-room.

"Miss Wilson wants you at once in San.," she said. "Come along—and when she's done with you," she added, "you may go and wash the ink off your hands. Your nails are simply disgusting!"

While Matron was away, Miss Wilson had brought water, sponge, and towel to the bedside and herself washed Jennifer's face so thoroughly that, for a minute or two, that young woman had to cease wailing. By the time she was drying the patient, a bewildered Blossom was standing at the door, wondering why on earth "Bill" wanted her in San.

"Bill" looked up and saw her. "Come here, Blossom," she said brusquely. "Now, Jennifer," she removed the towel from Jennifer's face. "Here's Blossom herself—and not a scratch anywhere on her! Stop that silly crying and look for yourself!"

Jennifer opened her eyes a slit. Then she shut them again with a gasp while the tears poured down her cheeks. This was too much for Blossom, who, despite all her faults, was a good-hearted girl.

She went up to the bed. "I say, Jenny," she said, "what under the sun is up with you? Don't howl like that, for goodness' sake!"

"O-o-oh!" Jennifer wailed, "it was my fault—all my fault!"

"*What* was your fault?" Blossom looked as she felt, completely bewildered.

"That you're all cut and your face spoilt for ever!" Jennifer ended with a kind of howl.

"*Cut*? I'm not cut at all! What on earth are you yattering about? You must be ravers!"

146

Jennifer shudderingly took her hands away from her face and this time looked properly—or at any rate as well as she could for tears. Blossom was standing beside her, her lovely face unmarked by the tiniest scratch, though her eyes were full of alarm.

"Now then, what d'you mean—*cut*?" she demanded, while Miss Wilson and Matron withdrew into the background—which meant the doorway—and left her to deal with the matter.

"But I *saw* you," Jennifer choked. "Your face was all cut to pieces and there was blood everywhere!"

"You *must* be ravers! There's not a thing the matter with me. Look at me!"

Blossom shoved up her short sleeves to the shoulder and then held up first one leg and then the other to show that there was not a mark on them.

Jennifer looked and drew a long, sobbing breath. "Oh, Blossom, I'm so *thankful*!"

"Well, that's smashing of you, of course, but I still don't see where you got your idea from nor why you've made such a fearful fuss."

"I—I thought you were cut and—and it would have been *my* fault."

"*Your* fault?" Blossom eyed her as if she were the prize freak of a circus show.

"Yes. It was me locked you into the art room."

So *that* mystery was solved! But before either of the startled pair in the doorway could say anything, Blossom had given them another shock.

"Oh—that! We rather guessed it was you. What an ass you are, Jennifer! I don't see what you expected to get by it."

Jennifer went scarlet. "I was mad with you because of what you said to me that night about slacking over the garden," she explained with sundry halts for sobs. "I meant to stop you being a reserve if I could."

"Well, that was a rotten thing to do all right," Blossom said calmly. "Didn't you think you'd be letting the school down if they needed me, you triple ass?"

Jennifer said nothing. She had been so obsessed by her hatred of Blossom that she had never given that side of the matter a thought until Blossom flung it at her like that.

"As a matter of fact," Blossom said, squatting down on

the side of the bed in complete defiance of rules, "it didn't really matter from that point of view, for Katharine was able to take my place. And did she do well! Oh, boy! I'm only sorry I wasn't there to see the whole thing! As for the locking-up business, you surely never imagined I'd stay put meek as Moses until someone came to let me out? You *are* a silly goat!"

"I'm—I'm most awfully sorry." Jennifer spoke low and she was crimson with shame.

"O.K.; that settles it and we'll say no more. But the next time you want to get back at anyone, just you *think* a bit before you do anything about it."

This, from Blossom, whose usual habit was to act first and think after, was too much for Miss Wilson. Clutching Matron's arm in a grip that nearly drew a squawk of protest from that lady, she got the pair of them out of the room, shut the door, dragged her startled coadjutor with her to the nearest dormitory and then dropped down on the first bed and gave rein to the shrieks of mirth she had been bottling up.

Matron looked at her. Then the humour of the whole affair struck her too, and for the next two or three minutes they simply let themselves go. So they never knew just how Blossom finally settled Jennifer.

When they had recovered themselves, however, Miss Wilson went back to find that persecuted person standing at the top of the stair, obviously waiting for her, and looking rather uncomfortable.

"Please, Miss Wilson," she said earnestly, "Jennifer's all right now. She said she felt sleepy, so I came away. And please, can I speak to you and Miss Annersley?"

"Miss Annerley is teaching just now. I think if you'll come to the study with me and tell me what you want to say I could repeat it to her and that would do."

Blossom looked doubtful. "Miss Wilson——"

"You come downstairs and tell me in comfort," the younger Head interrupted her firmly. "No—don't try to argue. It won't get you anywhere with me as you ought to know by this time."

Thereafter, Blossom held her tongue until they were in the study and she was standing opposite Miss Wilson, who waved her to a chair.

Blossom took no notice. She stood on one leg and rubbed the other foot down it.

"Well?" "Bill" asked.

"Why," Blossom said awkwardly, "I—I just wanted to say I've squared things up with Jennifer and—and can't you and Miss Annersley not take any notice of it now?"

"Your English, my good child, seems to stand in need of a little attention," Miss Wilson told her dispassionately. "I've a good mind to set you to parsing and analysing that last horrible sentence of yours! Now," having reduced her victim to a proper sense of humility, "suppose you begin at the beginning and tell the whole story."

Thus urged, Blossom told the story, slurring over as many details as she dared.

"Katharine and Hilary and I talked it over," she wound up, "and we decided it was probably Jennifer after the things I'd said to her about being a slacker. Then, as I'd rather asked for it, I thought I'd pipe down on it. Only she—I mean Jennifer—must have been having gory nightmares and she got all upset and—and—well, that was *it*, you see."

Miss Wilson did see. She also felt that Jennifer had had quite enough punishment with her nightmares to need no more. She knew that her co-Head would agree with that since, if it was possible to be lenient, Miss Annersley was. She was prepared to promise Blossom that Jennifer should not be further punished for her sins.

"But we must speak to her about it, Blossom," she pointed out. "I can promise you, though, that that will end it. You have both been very silly, thoughtless girls and I can't say I'm sorry either of you has suffered. It serves you both right. Now, the last bell rang some time ago and I hardly think it worth while to send you to whatever lesson it is for the last ten minutes, so you had better go upstairs and change and then go to the garden. You may tell Katharine and Hilary as you seem to have discussed it together, but I think we won't let anyone else know. Please ask those two to hold their tongues about it. Now you may go.—Oh, before you do I think I had better remind you that certain slang is not tolerated here. I suppose you don't want to put *all* your pocket-money into the fines-box?"

"No, Miss Wilson." Blossom blurted it out with a very red face. She bobbed her curtsy and made good her escape in short order, thankful to get away whole, so she told Katharine and Hilary later on.

CHAPTER XIX

A PAGEANT TO REMEMBER

FOR the next few weeks, the Chalet School had peace after such a stormy beginning to the term. Miss Annersley and Miss Wilson sighed with relief as week followed week and the girls attended to work, games, and their usual pastimes and everything went normally. Jennifer, finally forgiven, returned to Upper Fourth more subdued than anyone had ever known her before. Events had brought her up short and she seemed to have learned her lesson. At any rate, no one had any further complaints about her.

Blossom, too, contrived to be rather less heedless, which was all to the good. The prefects added "spiffing" to the list of forbidden slang, so it soon retired to the limbo of forgotten things whence Katharine's unguarded exclamation had recalled it.

As for Katharine herself, a long letter from Singapore, where her mother was recuperating from the effects of her imprisonment, rejoiced her heart. Word had come from her father, too, and Aunt Luce, learning that her sister-in-law meant to come home as soon as the doctors would permit it, remarked that in that case she was not likely to be needed, packed up her traps and disappeared into the wilds of Ireland in search of fresh objects for her brush.

Sir James Russell treated the school to a flying visit while he was at the Sanatorium among the Welsh Mountains and Dr Maynard, taking his place at the end of June, arrived at Carnbach to make arrangements for giving up Cartref, the house he had rented from Dickie Christy's father, since Plas Gwyn, the Maynard home, was now ready again for them.

He squeezed in a long week-end on St Briavel's and brought all the latest news from Canada. The Russell twins were big healthy babies, he said, and all the other children were well and strong. As for Jo herself, a few weeks of doing nothing but rest and enjoy herself, coupled with the stimulating climate of Canada, had worked wonders with her, and he solemnly assured her friends that she was her own saucy self once more.

He was remaining in England until the schools broke up as he was escorting David, the eldest of the Russell family, to Canada for the summer holidays. Lady Russell had been sixteen months without sight of her firstborn and refused to let any more time pass before she saw him again. So David was to fly over with his uncle, much to the envy of his cousin Rix Bettany, Peggy's twin brother.

"Dr Jack," as the school called him, also brought a pageant which Jo had written for them to perform at the end of term. The excitements of half-term and the expedition in honour of Lady Russell's birthday which finally turned out to be a trip by sea to Bideford and Barnstaple, were first got out of the way and then the Staff set to work to cast the pageant and begin rehearsals.

The school generally gave some sort of garden show for the Prize Giving at the end of the summer term, but this time Jo had provided them with a water pageant. She remarked airily in her accompanying letter that she saw no reason for not making all possible use of Kittiwake Cove, their own private bathing place, and had ransacked Lemprière's Classical Dictionary for everything she could find about Neptune, Amphitrite, and all the Oceanides.

"Let's hope it's a decent day," Miss Wilson said gloomily as she skimmed through the book of words. "Otherwise, we'll have had it! We couldn't possibly do this sort of thing in any hall."

"Jo mentions that," Miss Annersley replied, looking up the lengthy screed she was reading. "She says that in the event of it's proving too wet or too rough for a sea pageant, we must turn it into a concert and use the songs and dances for that. She also says," she went on, reading aloud:

"At the same time, I don't suppose there's any need to worry. I've thought back, and honestly, I can't remember one wet day for Parents' Day, and only one that you could call windy. I expect it'll be all right.

"I'm giving my usual Margot Venables prize and you can tap Jack for the cash. I've given him due warning.

"Madge and Jem have definitely renewed the lease of this place for a further nine months, so you aren't likely to see me or the children much before April next year. We're all quite fit and well. Charles is improving every day and has actually began to put a little flesh on his bones!

"Robin arrived last week. She has lost her cough, thank goodness, and though she's thinner than I like, Jem has vetted her and he says she's perfectly sound, only there must be no more settlement work. What she will do now, I'm not very sure. I have my own ideas, but I'm saying no more for the moment. After all, it's *her* life."

"What on earth is she driving at?" Miss Wilson demanded. "Has Robin developed a young man by any chance?"

"You know as much as I," her friend retorted. "Everyone *says* that T.B. isn't hereditary, but I know that Jem has always hoped she wouldn't marry After all, her mother died of it and there has always been the fear for her."

Miss Wilson nodded as she thought of the early days when Robin, Jo's adopted sister and everyone's darling, had been a pitifully frail little mortal. The strict regime to which the doctors at the Sanatorium, then in the Tirolean Alps, had subjected her, had effected a great change. A year's settlement work after she had left Oxford had brought back a threat of the old trouble and Robin had spent ten months in Switzerland.

"Let's hope Canada does as much for her as it seems to have done for Margot and the rest," she said soberly.

"It probably will," Miss Annersley replied. Then the subject was dropped.

From then until the last week, what with rehearsals, examinations, sports, a regatta at which Katharine distinguished herself by winning five prizes, not to speak of Guides and all their usual multifarious occupations, the girls found no time for specialised mischief.

By the time Parents' Day came, everyone was in a state of wild excitement and Miss Wilson had to issue a ukase against tapping the barometer to see if it were going up or not. Otherwise, as she complained, its balance would be destroyed for ever!

As Jo Maynard had foretold, they were favoured with a glorious day, with the sun shining brilliantly, and just enough of a breeze to temper the heat. Prize Giving would take place in the garden at eleven; lunch would follow; then the Pageant was to begin at two, which gave the girls time to change and rush the light forms and chairs down to the shore for the audience.

The big excitement of the Prize Giving was the winner of the Margot Venables prize. This had been instituted by Jo Maynard a few years before and was awarded to the girl who obtained most votes from the entire school—Staff as well as girls—for being kind, helpful, and unselfish. Until the actual voting had taken place, no one ever knew who was likely to win it, so there was reason for the girls' excitement.

Miss Annersley knew it and was merciful. When she rose to read the annual report, she said, "Before I begin, I should like to announce that the winner of the Margot Venables prize this year is Tom Gay, who polled almost two-thirds of the votes. Well done, Tom!"

Tom reddened to the roots of her short wavy hair and the school applauded lustily until the Head's lifted hand hushed them. After that, Prize Giving followed its usual course. Lunch began at twelve-fifteen, after which those who had elaborate dresses to get into fled to change, while the others took the forms and chairs down to Kittiwake Cove and disposed them to one side where a little shade flung by the tall cliffs would add greatly to the comfort of the audience. Then they, too, sped off to change.

By ten to two, the entire audience was seated and being entertained by all the Staff not on duty. At two o'clock prompt, strains of soft music rose from behind some nearby rocks and then a stream of sea-fairies emerged, moving in a mazy dance. They were clad in floating draperies of greens, blues, and soft yellow, with here and there a white or dark brown, and as they weaved in and out, singing "Come Unto these Yellow Sands" to a charming setting composed by Margia Stevens, an old girl of the school and a well-known pianist, those watching were enchanted.

The song ended, they formed into graceful groups, all slightly turned to look back along the shore to a further great rock rising out of the water. Fresh music arose, faintly at first, then swelling out as a sort of barge appeared, towed by three of the school's boats. All four were decked with seaweeds, shells, and draperies, and the rowers wore short belted tunics of every colour imaginable. An orchestra sat in the prow of the barge, and amidships was King Neptune, Queen Amphitrite, and all the court.

King Neptune—Dickie Christy—wore a short tunic of green over blue trunks and carried a gilded trident. A crown of cardboard starfish adorned his head and he had a magnificent green beard flowing to his waist. Beside him on the throne which was backed by a nautilus shell made of stiff muslin stretched over wires and painted in rainbow colours, sat Amphitrite—Peggy Bettany—in blue and white. Her crown was an elaborate coral necklace belonging to her mother and she wore strings of coral round her neck and twisted round wrists and ankles.

Tom Gay played Triton, gorgeous in blue and gold, with an immense conch-shell held to her lips every now and then. This gentleman stood to one side of the throne and on the other was Arion, equally gorgeous in crimson and silver, and carrying a cardboard and string lyre, lavishly gilded and wreathed with strings of pearl beads.

Round the feet of these magnificent creatures were clustered the sea nymphs in gauzy white robes, decked with green and blue, and as the transformed old tub, which was actually the potato boat belonging to the Dominican Priory on a near-by island, drew near the shore, all joined in singing "Sea Shells", a quaint old song from the early part of the last century which Jo had unearthed from somewhere.

The Staff watched the stately approach of the barge with some trepidation lest the rowers should bring it too far inshore and ground it; but the girls had been well drilled and while they were still at a safe enough distance, the anchors were dropped and the progress was stayed.

Neptune rose to his feet and proceeded to deliver a speech of welcome to the visitors in a deep bass voice! — Dickie said later that she felt a complete fool with all that face fungus and as a result produced her voice from her sandals.

It went down splendidly with the guests, but one or two of the junior Staff hastily retired to hide their guffaws, and small Janice Chester very nearly forgot her part in the shock of hearing Dickie Christy suddenly speaking in a man's voice.

Verity-Anne Carey, who was also one of the fairies, kept her head, however, and gave Janice a shove, hissing, "Go on! Call them ashore!"

Janice danced forward, dropped in a very low curtsy and, maintaining her position very precariously, said in her clear little voice, "Oh, Neptune, favour thy subjects by a visit to these sands that we may rejoice this summer day."

At the same moment, half a dozen Nereids appeared, leading an enormous cart-horse, of whom his owner had said that if you let off a bomb under him, he would just twitch an ear and go on calmly.

The Nereids plunged into the sea—they all wore green swimming-suits, hung with ribbons of seaweed—and the great creature ambled amiably along in their midst. Neptune and Amphitrite walking along a gangway run out from the boat, mounted him and he was turned round and led to shore. The remainder of the court were brought off by the other two school boats which suddenly appeared round the cliff.

Arrived on the beach, Neptune leapt down from his steed, lifted his queen from her perch, and led her to the big rock which had been transformed into a throne; while the Nereids took the horse back to his owner who took charge of him until he was needed again.

Now various groups came to offer their loyalty to the sea king. Some sturdy sailors danced an energetic hornpipe, followed by others who sang the sea shanties "Johnny Come Down from Hilo" and "Shanadar" with great sweetness.

The sea nymphs and Nereids—the latter now changed into sea-hued draperies, too—produced rainbow-hued scarves and performed a graceful little ballet. Arion—Nancy Chester—the possessor of a lovely contralto voice, stood forward and sang "Where Corals Lie," accompanied by the orchestra who were all got up as mermaids and had had to be carried ashore! Only the two 'cellists had feet and not the silver-painted sacking tails which adorned the rest.

Then Neptune prayed his queen to honour the court with a song, and Peggy, who had a charming mezzo-soprano voice though it was of no great strength, stood up and sang Margia Stevens' setting of those lines from "The Forsaken Merman" which describe the home of the sea kings.

Finally, Dickie arose to deliver the last speech. She had

recovered her self-possession by this time, and it was her own voice which gave Jo's closing words.

"And now our duties call us to our home
Deep 'neath the sparkling waters of the sea.
Our merry playtime's ended, and we go
To call the waves, the tides, the springs, the rivers.
And all things watery to their wonted tasks.
Come, my fair queen, and come, my faithful followers!
Back to the depths of ocean we must go.
My son, my gallant Triton, wind thy horn:
Summon our steed to bear us to our barge.
    And so, farewell!
                    Oh, may this day's brief sport
Deepen the love a nation, born to fare
Forth on our mighty waters, bears the sea.
Come, Amphitrite! Come, ye happy nymphs
And sportive Nereids! And, my songful poet,
My music-loving Arion, come with us,
And let sweet sounds attend our parting here."

Led by Triton, his conch-shell held to his lips, the procession formed up and Neptune and his queen followed with stately tread, hand in hand, the Nereids racing to the rocks to cast off their draperies and retrieve the horse, while the nymphs drifted after their monarchs and the fairies resumed their opening dance as the unseen musicians swept into the music again.

The faithful steed arrived and Amphitrite mounted him from a flat rock on the shore. Neptune vaulted up behind her and reached forward for the reins. They were about to set off, when Triton, who had been very careful up to this, suddenly forgot himself and blew heavily into his conch.

The results can be better imagined than described. The horse had certainly never heard such an appalling sound in all his nineteen years. He flattened his ears, wrenched his head free from the hold of the startled Nereids, two of whom went head over heels into the water, and turned and galloped madly down the shore with Neptune and

156

Amphitrite clinging to his mane—Peggy was very slight, and big Dickie had long arms, fortunately!

One of the nymphs, in the act of stepping on to the rock ready for the ferrying boats, jumped violently and nearly went over into the sea, saving herself by grabbing at Arion, who almost overbalanced and only saved the pair of them by a series of contortions that, Hilary Burn declared later, would have done credit to a professional contortionist.

The horse's master lost *his* head and tore along the beach at the best pace of which he was capable, shouting, "Woa there—woa there!" to which the frightened animal paid not the slightest attention.

Mercifully, Dickie had managed to keep hold of the reins and the elderly horse, finding that he could not keep up his burst of speed with the two girls on his back, came to his senses in time to avoid any serious trouble and allowed Neptune to turn him so that the ocean monarchs were able to trot back to the rock in a very much more dignified style than they had left it. The sea-nymphs had kept their heads, thanks mainly to Nita Eltringham and Anthea Barnett, so that they, too, reached the barge in safety.

The people who came best out of it were the fairies, who attended to their dance with a concentration born of the fact that it needed all their attention to keep their weaving right and who took themselves off as beautifully as they had brought themselves on.

Once it was clear that there was no danger, the audience simply let itself go and screamed with laughter. Warned by Miss Lawrence, the orchestra broke into the national anthem and the school began to sing. By the time that was ended, most folk had recovered themselves, though here and there were people who kept chuckling over the unexpected end to the Pageant.

Stout, pretty Mrs Bettany was one of them. She sat gurgling and mopping her eyes alternately until her very shocked Bride descended on her and demanded to know what she thought she was doing.

"Peg and Dick might have had a very nasty accident," Bride said severely. "*I* don't see anything to laugh at!"

Mrs Bettany wiped her eyes for the last time. "Sure, I knew they were safe enough. I'd be sorry to think a daughter of *mine* couldn't manage an old house-end like that without much trouble. The poor beast! 'Twas enough to give him his end! However did Tom manage to make such a noise?"

"It was a conch-shell," Bride explained. "We tried it out ages ago and everyone said she mustn't really blow through it, it makes such a ghastly row."

"Tom must have taken leave of her senses," Polly Winterton, who had come up with Bride, declared.

"Auntie Jo would be ravers if she knew the mess-up of the end of her pageant," Bride added.

" 'Twill be a good tale to tell in my next letter," her mother responded. "Well, we must be off or we shall miss our train and Daddy is meeting Mrs Winterton and myself at Cardiff so we mustn't keep him waiting. Good-bye, Bride, until next Thursday. Where's my baby?"

Small Maeve bobbed up to say good-bye and then the two ladies went to join the big cobble that was taking visitors round to the landing-stage while the girls climbed the cliff-path to school.

Tom, when taxed with her crime, was most apologetic. She had never meant to blow really hard, but she thought just one, tiny breath into the conch wouldn't hurt.

"Well, if that's what you call a tiny breath, I wouldn't like to be within earshot when you make a real effort," Peggy said severely.

Katharine was looking forward to spending the summer holidays with Hilary Wilson, but she never went. On the Wednesday, the Carnbach ferry brought a thin, sallow-faced lady to St Briavel's and after she had had a brief conversation with the two Heads of the Chalet School, they left her, and Katharine was sent to the study. When she came in, she looked round and then her eyes lit up as she saw a well-remembered smile. She hurled herself on the stranger with a wild cry of "Mother! Oh, Mother *darling*!" and a rapturous hug bridged the long years of parting.

Mrs Gordon had reached England in safety; and, best of all good news, the Chinese Government had unexpectedly released Dr Gordon, and he was now in Hong Kong awaiting transport to England.

"So I've got them both safe again," Katharine told the dormitory that night as she sat up in bed, hugging her knees. "Mother won't go out again—or not until I'm grown-up; and he may not, either. Isn't it gorgeous?

Wasn't I right to hang on and trust in God? I'm coming back next term and I'm to be here until my schooldays end. Then, if I still want to be a Games mistress—and you bet I shall!—it'll mean Bedford or Chelsea or somewhere. But at least I'll belong to this school."

"And that might never have happened," Hilary Wilson reminded her, "if your Aunt Luce hadn't made uch a mull of things and sent you to the *wrong* Chalet School!"

Armadas are chosen by children all over the world. They're designed to fit your pocket, and your pocket money too — and they make terrific presents for friends. They're colourful, exciting, and there are hundreds of titles to choose from — thrilling mysteries, spooky horror stories, hilarious joke books, brain-teasing puzzles, fascinating hobby books, stories about ponies and schools — and many, many more. Armada has something for everyone.

Book Tokens

Give them
the pleasure of choosing
Book Tokens can be bought
and exchanged at most
bookshops

Armada